A Rex Graves Mystery

MURDER
IN THE RAW

C.S. Challinor

MIDNIGHT INK
WOODBURY, MINNESOTA

First Edition
First Printing, 2009

Book design and format by Donna Burch
Cover design by Gavin Dayton Duffy
Cover art sunglasses © Comstock
Editing by Connie Hill

Midnight Ink, an imprint of Llewellyn Publications

Library of Congress Cataloging-in-Publication Data

Challinor, C. S. (Caroline S.)
  Murder in the raw : a rex graves mystery / by C. S. Challinor. — 1st ed.
    p. cm.
  ISBN 978-0-7387-1439-4
  1. Missing persons—Investigation—Fiction. 2. Nudist camps—Fiction. 3. West Indies, French—Fiction. I. Title.
  PS3603.H3366M87   2009
  813'.6—dc22   2008051073

Midnight Ink
Llewellyn Publications
2143 Wooddale Drive, Dept. 978-0-7387-1439-4
Woodbury, MN 55125-2989 USA
www.midnightinkbooks.com

Printed in the United States of America

CAST OF MAIN CHARACTERS IN ORDER OF APPEARANCE

REX GRAVES, sleuth—the Scots barrister flies to a nudist resort in the French West Indies to investigate a young celebrity's disappearance

PASCAL, limo driver at the Plage d'Azur Resort

LT. LATOUR, police officer in charge at the local commissariat

MONSIEUR BIJOU, an influential developer with hedonistic tastes

GREG HASTINGS, manager of the Plage d'Azur Resort

HELEN D'ARCY, who takes a Caribbean cruise in a hopeful pursuit of Rex Graves

JEAN-LUC VALQUEZ, a rising star on the French stage

GUESTS AT THE PLAGE D'AZUR RESORT

SABINE DURAND, captivating French actress who disappears mysteriously

PAUL and ELIZABETH WINSLOW, new owners of the Swanmere Manor Hotel in England, who ask Rex Graves to take on the case

BROOKLYN T. CHALMERS, self-made millionaire and international playboy

VERNON POWELL, hardnosed New York entertainment lawyer married to the actress

DR. VON MUELLER, wife MARTINA, and daughter GABY from Vienna, Austria

DAVID and ANTONIA WEEKS, proprietors of the French School of Cordon Bleu in London; the exotic beauty "Toni" is no fan of Sabine

DUKE and PAM FARLEY, oily Texas tycoon and his trophy wife

DICK and PENNY IRVING, promoters of health, fitness, and naturism, from Toronto

SEAN and NORA O'SULLIVAN, founders of the Coolidge Theatre in Dublin

ST. MARTIN, FRENCH WEST INDIES

TESTIMONY OF DAVID WEEKS

It is unbelievable that Sabine Durand is dead. She was the essence of our group, the lingering perfume, if you will. Whenever I evoke St. Martin, it is always Sabine I conjure up in my memory.

I often saw her walking at dusk along the shore, always alone. Our beach cabana is the last of eight before the promontory of rocks begins on the eastern side. She would have had to climb those rocks to get to the strand of beach beyond, but she was agile enough, I suppose. In any case, there was no other access except by boat. People sometimes dock their catamarans on that side, but since you can sunbathe nude all along La Plage d'Azur, there really isn't any point in going over there unless you want to "do it" au naturel. People, after all, pay big money to be seen in the buff at La Plage.

We've been coming to St. Martin for ten years now. You end up synchronizing your holiday with other couples. It's always the same crowd in July: Paul and Elizabeth Winslow, Dick and Penny Irving, the O'Sullivans, the von Muellers, the Farleys ... Duke Farley has been bringing his new wife, Pam, the last couple of years, so I suppose it's not exactly the same crowd as before. Brooklyn Chalmers brought a girlfriend two years ago, but not this time around. And, of course, Vernon and Sabine. July is by far and away the best time. August is Swingers' Month and come September you run into hurricane season.

I don't know whether we'll return next year. It won't be the same without Sabine, and I doubt Vernon will come back, poor fellow. He must feel dreadfully guilty. After all, he never accompanied his wife on her walks, though I think she preferred it that way. She was remote and mysterious. I think that was part of the allure. She drew people like moths to a candle. You wanted to protect her from singeing her wings sort of thing. Well, the others will say the same, I'm sure.

Sabine always wore the diaphanous white pareo on her walks. She would have taken it off before she went for a swim, which would explain why part of it was found by the rocks. But she wouldn't have gone for a dip right before dinner. I don't go for the shark theory—she would have known better than to go swimming at dusk. Then again, she never was the sort of person to do what you'd expect. More likely a stalker was involved; actresses often attract that sort.

It must have been just after six p.m. on Tuesday 10th when I saw her for the last time on her walk. We usually all meet at

2

seven for drinks at The Cockatoo. My wife and I sometimes
escorted Sabine to the restaurant on her way back, but it was
Paul Winslow's birthday, and we didn't want to be late, so we
left our cabana in good time. We never saw Sabine again.
Those are my recollections of the night in question.

Signed,
David Weeks

ONE

REX GRAVES RESTED THE testimony on his knees, which, much to his aggravation, bumped the seat in front, even though he was in recline mode. White ridges of clouds floated outside the airplane window, while inside the first class cabin the mutedly excited voices of vacationers arose all around him. He checked his watch: another hour before they landed at Juliana Airport. He waved over the flight attendant and ordered a second Glenfiddich on the rocks before settling down to extrapolate the pertinent information from David Weeks' flowery statement.

He wondered again about the people with whom he would be spending the next few weeks at the request of the Winslows, the new owners of the Swanmere Manor Hotel in southern England where he had solved his first case. Sabine Durand had mysteriously disappeared while they were together on their annual vacation on St. Martin, and they'd asked Rex to fly over, all expenses paid, to look into the matter.

Paul Winslow, who suspected foul play, had persuaded the local Gendarmerie to fax over the statements of all the guests present at the resort on the night Sabine went missing. The von Muellers had been at the airport meeting their daughter off an Air France flight and had not returned until late, and consequently, their statements had not been taken. The Irvings from Canada had taken a day trip to the neighboring island of St. Barts, arriving back at the resort at some time in the evening.

Winslow had explained it was only due to the intervention of a certain Monsieur Bijou, an influential developer on the island, that the gendarmes had deigned to draw up a missing person's report at all. As it was, they had not arrived until the following morning, and the two detectives from the Police Judiciary had not taken the statements until two days later. Rex swirled the ice cubes in the bottom of his tumbler, reflecting that any evidence, including footprints, would have been badly compromised by the time the gendarmes arrived, and the guests would have had time to work on their alibis—assuming one or more among them was guilty.

According to Winslow, the gendarme report cited the recovery of a gold ankle bracelet, identified by the guests as having belonged to Sabine Durand, and a strip of bloody gauze, apparently from the white pareo referred to in Weeks' testimony. The husband's cell phone had been retrieved in the vicinity of the secluded beach.

Until Rex visited the spot and interviewed the guests himself, he couldn't begin to draw any conclusions as to what might have happened to the young actress.

"We'll be landing momentarily," the flight attendant said, relieving him of his empty glass.

The plane executed an arc above an ocean of shimmering blues and greens. A crowd of spectators slid into view on the palm-dotted beach, faces uplifted as the 757 skimmed over them before touching down on the landing strip. When the plane taxied to a stop, Rex let out a sigh of relief. Fear of flying was second only to his fear of the water, and it had been with a tightness in his gut that he had said goodbye to his son in Miami after a brief stopover from Scotland.

Gathering his luggage, he joined the line of passengers in the aisle and inched his way to the plane exit. A breeze ruffled his short-sleeved shirt, a welcome change to the muggy heat he had left just hours before in Florida.

This'll do me just fine, he thought as he contemplated the buildings clustered on volcanic hills overlooking the rippling expanse of the Caribbean. He imagined a pirate sloop moored in one of the bays, a Jolly Roger billowing from the topmast.

Only when he discovered his suitcase had not followed him onto the plane did his sunny mood cloud over briefly.

The clerk at the lost baggage counter handed him a pack of emergency toiletries. "If you leave the number of your hotel, we'll call when it arrives."

"I'm staying at the *Plage d'Azur* on the French side."

"Oh, you won't be needing clothes there," the clerk assured him.

"What d'you mean?"

"It's a naturist hotel."

"A what?"

"Clothing is optional."

"Optional?"

Why had Paul Winslow not thought to mention that little detail? Did he think Rex's Scottish Presbyterian sensibilities would be offended by the prospect of public nudity?

Aye, it might have influenced my decision to come, he conceded as he made his way out of the terminal, holding on to the word "optional."

Optional meant he had a choice.

A man in the crowd held up a sign with "REX GRAVES" in bold letters. A welcoming smile cracked his walnut-brown face. He had a youthful expression and the whitest teeth Rex had ever seen, though he might have been forty.

"I'm Pascal, da hotel driver."

"Pleased to meet you. How far to the resort?"

"Depends on traffic. It be at the other end of da island. You got a suitcase?"

"It went AWOL. This is all I have." Rex held up his briefcase and carry-on. "Fortunately I have a change of clothes in this bag."

"You won't be needing dem," the driver said, taking the bag and leading Rex out the exit. "Ev'rybody go about buck naked at da resort." In the parking lot, he opened the trunk of a shiny minivan and installed the sparse luggage.

"Mind if I sit up front with you?" Rex asked, never one to miss an opportunity to find out as much as he could about where he was going.

"Sure. It be just da two of us. No more guests be arriving now till August." The driver held open the passenger door. "Which cabana you staying in?"

"Number one—with Brooklyn Chalmers."

"Real nice American gentleman. You been to St. Martin before?" Pascal asked, hopping in beside him.

"This is my first time to the Caribbean."

"Where your accent from?"

"Scotland."

Pascal started the van. "Never had nobody from Scotland before. There be a couple from Ireland an' two couples from England. Mostly we get Americans. The Irvings be from Canada. They got piercings ev'rywhere. And I mean *ev'rywhere.*"

Rex thought about this for a moment. "Ouch," he said.

"Da young lady dat went missing from da resort went to school in England," Pascal continued, turning onto the main road. "But she lived in Paris. Mr. Winslow tol' me you was investigating her disappearance. He say to take good care of you. So you need anyting, Mr. Graves, anyting at all, you jus' holler." He grinned broadly.

They passed a quarry and several car rental agencies.

"What can you tell me about the island?" Rex asked.

"We be going to da northeastern part. Dis here da Dutch side. Da capital be Philipsburg, named after Cap'n John Philips, a Scotsman in da Dutch Navy all da way back in the 1700s."

"A Scotsman? Very gratifying," Rex said with smug pride, feeling more at home now in the narrow streets of the suburb, where rickety second-story verandas jutted out from pastel-colored houses. Pretty island girls with beaded braids toted wicker baskets laden with tropical fruit on their hips. Rex craned his neck for a better view.

Native pedestrians assumed right of way over the small, dusty cars on the road. What few signs existed were bilingual, and Rex had yet to see a traffic light.

"Christopher Columbus discovered da island on da date of da Feast of St. Martin," Pascal recited, sounding as though he had given the tour at least a dozen times before.

A border sign in French welcomed them to the northern half of the island. Pascal explained that this side was an overseas territory of France. Rex sincerely hoped he wouldn't be called upon to use his execrable schoolboy French during his stay. The thought of having to flounder through the intricacies of Gallic grammar while standing there starkers was the stuff of nightmares.

His worst fears materialized when, half an hour later, the minivan turned into the resort.

"*Soyez le bienvenu!*" a naked Paul Winslow greeted him from the main entrance, waving a crusty baguette in the air.

TWO

REX SHOOK WINSLOW'S HAND. "Good to see you again."

The first and last time Rex had seen him, at a reception held for the acquisition of the Swanmere Manor Hotel, Paul Winslow wore a dinner jacket. He had a pleasant face, with graying hair beginning to recede at the temples, and stood five feet nine, his pale English skin reddened to the hue of a boiled lobster. Rex made a mental note to slather on sun cream while he was here. He didn't want to end up with his skin matching his hair.

"They have a shop off reception where you can buy an assortment of French delicacies," Winslow continued in English. "This bread is delivered daily. Sorry I couldn't meet you off the plane myself, but Elizabeth took the car into Marigot. Did you see your son Campbell on your way over?"

"Aye. He's so tanned I hardly recognized him. He's spending part of the summer in Miami with his girlfriend." A rich Cuban beauty who looked like she had just stepped off a fashion runway.

The driver took Rex's luggage out of the van, and they followed him down a sandy path to a wooden cabana resembling a chalet, the first in a shallow semicircle of eight built right on the beach.

"How are the renovations coming along at the Manor?" Rex asked Winslow.

"Pretty well. It was a last-minute decision to come to St. Martin, but as Elizabeth pointed out, it'll be a while before we can get away once the hotel reopens. The contractor is a reliable fellow and we felt we could leave the work in his hands for a month."

Pascal waited for them on the porch.

"Here we are." Winslow opened the front door onto a tiled hallway. "We typically don't lock our doors. There's a safe in your bedroom for valuables, and two guards patrol the resort."

"Is there much crime on the island?"

"Theft is a problem, but none has been reported at the resort in over a year. All the same, it's a good idea to keep your cell phone locked up. You can't use it on the premises anyway."

"Why not?"

"It's considered a breach of privacy, old fellow. Cell phones can take photos and videos. This is a nudist resort, after all."

"Aye, I wanted to ask you about that." Rex tipped the driver and he left. "I hope euros are okay."

"Euros, dollars, it's all viable currency here." Winslow led him into the open living and kitchen area where glass sliders offered a panoramic vista of powdery white sand, coconut palms, and turquoise sea. Everyone outside was naked. "You must be dying to get out of your clothes," he said.

"I'm not sure I want to wander about in the altogether."

"Oh, you'll get used to it. Comes a point where it seems silly bothering with clothes. Just do what you're comfortable with." Rex averted his eyes as the nude man bent to open the fridge door. "Brook said he left you a stock of beer in case you arrived before he got back. I told him you were a Guinness man. Would you like one?"

"Aye, thanks." The can perspired cold droplets in Rex's hand. He took a few gulps and exhaled. "That's better," he said.

Winslow helped himself to a Heineken. "I hope you'll get on all right with Brook. He's very personable, really. The other alternative would have been to have you room with Vernon, but he's still in a state of shock and probably needs his space, even though it's been a week since Sabine disappeared."

"Was he very fond of his wife?"

"Crazy about her, although there were arguments between them. She was a very beautiful woman and, naturally, Vernon got jealous over all the attention she received. Sometimes I think she provoked it."

"Provoked his jealousy?"

"I think she liked to see how far she could go and led men on just for the fun of it. Wouldn't surprise me if Vernon snapped that night and wanted to teach her a lesson. I'm not saying he necessarily meant to kill her."

"How long had they been married?"

"Seven years. She was a young thing of twenty-one when they wed. He's thirty years older."

"Something would have had to happen to make him snap enough to kill her after seven years." Rex crushed the can in his hand. "Do they recycle here?"

"Good God, you're a powerful chap. Lost some weight since I saw you, didn't you? Yes, there's a recycling bin outside the main building, by the Laundromat, or you can just leave it for maid service." Winslow hesitated before adding, "I ought to mention that some of us believe Sabine and Brook were having an affair."

"Was Vernon aware of it?"

"Not sure, but he started acting quite frostily toward Brook. If Brook and Sabine were having it away, they were quite discreet about it."

"Any suspects other than the husband?"

Winslow examined the green bottle in his hand. "I don't want to tell tales out of school—I just want to get to the bottom of this. When Sabine disappeared, my wife thought you might be the man to help. Not to put too fine a point on it, we're all successful businessmen here, and you can understand what makes us tick. It won't be too much like having a stranger among us."

"You think it was one of the guests?"

"A guard patrols the beach at night and he didn't see any non-resorters up at this end. If there was a struggle, as the blood on the pareo fragment suggests, it's more likely the assailant was a man, don't you think?"

"Possibly. Does this security guard work for the resort?"

"Yes. Another one patrols the gate and walks around the outer perimeter. They're very unobtrusive, and it gives the guests a sense of security."

Rex had noticed a man in a khaki uniform when the driver pulled up in front of reception.

"Well, I'll leave you to it," Winslow said. "This is the best time of the day for a dip. The water's warm and the sun's not too hot."

"What's the average temperature?"

"Low eighties, but the trade winds cool things off. I'll swing by at seven and take you to The Cockatoo to meet the others. David Weeks can't wait to make your acquaintance."

Rex couldn't wait to meet him either, nor any of the other suspects. "Aye, see you then, Paul. And thanks for your hospitality."

"Think nothing of it. You're not just here to work, you know." Winslow picked up his baguette from the counter and saluted him with it.

When he had left, Rex entered the bedroom where Pascal had deposited his bag and briefcase. He hung up his change of clothes in the wall closet and, upon rummaging in his bag, realized he must have foolishly packed his trunks in the missing suitcase.

Och, the heck with it, he said to himself, stripping out of his clothes.

Wrapping a white bath towel around his waist, he drew back the mosquito screen in the living room and stepped onto the back porch.

A sandy trail led through clumps of sea grape to the water. The beach formed a two-mile crescent around the bay where a tri-catamaran and a couple of sailboats bobbed on the blue surface. Beneath lurked darker patches of seaweed. On the sand, yellow umbrellas resembling inverted sunflowers shaded nude bathers on their lounge-chairs. The concession serviced the entire beach, which was open to the public, but the yellow chairs and umbrellas, as Rex had been informed, were free to resort guests.

A soft contour of hills formed a backdrop to a village of bars and boutiques at the far end of the beach. In the opposite direction, beyond the resort and boat rental shack, lay the promontory where Sabine's ankle bracelet and pareo fragment had been found.

Satisfied that no one was paying him the least bit of attention, Rex discarded his towel on a lounge chair by the water and waded into the shallows. The sea, warm and refreshing, washed away the strain of the day spent traveling. He swam out to an anchored sunbathing raft and, hoisting himself up the ladder, surveyed the island at the mouth of the bay and wondered if reef sharks ventured this close to shore. He swam back in a hurry.

At the beach, he grabbed his towel and covered himself up with lightning speed. Engrossed in books and magazines and in conversation with other nudists, no one so much as looked in his direction. After returning to the cabana, he showered and changed into his spare shirt and lightweight pants. He would join the others for drinks at The Cockatoo, but he'd be damned if he would undress for the occasion.

Seated on the patio, cold beer in hand, he perused Mrs. Weeks' statement to see how it compared to her husband's.

I last saw Sabine Durand on Tuesday, July 10. We had gone over to the Dutch side of the island for shopping—Sabine, Elizabeth Winslow, Nora O'Sullivan, and myself. Martina von Mueller did not join us on this occasion since she was meeting her daughter at the airport. The Canadian couple had left on a sightseeing trip to St. Barts early that morning. Pam Farley stayed behind at the resort for a massage and facial.

Philipsburg is a mob scene when the cruise ships dock, so we always avoid Wednesdays. I bought a silk pareo. The Cockatoo is a nudist restaurant, but there is an unvoiced etiquette that requires diners to sit on something, even if it is only one's towel. And, of course, bringing a beach towel to dinner is hardly appropriate. The men wear wraps. A bit silly if you ask me. It looks like they're wearing aprons, and you would never catch David wearing an apron at home. He says he spends enough time in one at his school of French cuisine.

Our daughter bought him a Male Chauvinist Pig apron one Christmas as a joke. She was about eleven at the time and, of course, we all laughed. Anyway, talking of male chauvinist pigs, the men ate out of Sabine's hand. She had that effect on men. The young French waiters at The Cockatoo were always tripping over each other to serve her. Sabine would just laugh in her childlike way, and everyone would laugh right along with her.

Going back to the other day in Philipsburg ... I bought a Delft china spoon holder and some linen napkins. Sabine, as I recall, treated herself to a tortoiseshell compact in the shape of a scallop. We had lunch in town, and the hotel limo picked us up at four o'clock as arranged. I went back to my cabana to rest. David and the other men from the group had gone on a scuba dive that day. They didn't get back until six. David had a touch of the sun, so I made him stay in and drink lots of water until it was time to go to The Cockatoo for Paul's forty-sixth birthday dinner. Sabine never appeared.

At ten p.m., we called the gendarmes, but they didn't arrive until the next morning as they were busy with a burglary in Grand Case. The hotel sent two guards out to the rocks. It was dark even with flashlights, but they found a cell phone

belonging to Sabine's husband. We searched all over the resort.
I can't imagine what might have happened to her.

This, I believe, is an accurate account of everything I know
relating to Ms. Durand's disappearance.

Antonia ("Toni") Weeks

Contrary to her husband's testimony, which Rex had read on
the plane, Toni Weeks' voluble statement showed no emotion over
the loss of a friend. Her husband owned the famous French School
of Cordon Bleu in London and, according to Paul Winslow, they
had known Sabine Durand before she went on the stage.

The rest of the guests' statements were in the same vein. The
men tended to wax lyrical while, of the women's statements, only
Elizabeth Winslow's, written in an elegant hand, indicated any dis-
tress over Sabine Durand's disappearance. He had met Mrs. Winslow at the Swanmere Manor banquet: a tall redhead who must
have been a knockout in her youth.

"Hey," declared an American voice behind him. "Oh—sorry,
didn't mean to startle you."

Twisting around in his chair, Rex saw a man in his mid-thirties,
good build, average height—and, mercifully, wearing shorts. Dark-
haired and devilishly handsome, this couldn't be other than Brooklyn. Winslow had given him thumbnail descriptions of all the
guests at the Plage d'Azur Resort. Rex half stood and, introducing
himself, shook hands.

The newcomer exuded an air of confidence, his smoky green
eyes appraising Rex with frank interest. "Brooklyn T. Chalmers.
Everybody calls me Brook."

Did Sabine? Rex decided to defer asking him about the level of intimacy between him and the missing woman. In spite of his easy manner, he was clearly not a man to be trifled with. President of the Brooklyn Trust in Manhattan, Chalmers was a self-made millionaire who had piloted himself to the island in his Malibu Piper and raced cars professionally, with a best finish of third at the Indy 500 last year.

"Thanks for putting me up."

"No problem. Sorry I wasn't here earlier. Had to fly to Aruba. Can I get you another beer?"

"No, thanks. It must be amazing to pilot your own plane."

Brooklyn sat down with a bottle of mineral water. "I can fly out to the islands whenever I get the time, without the hassle of major airports. We have a branch office in the Bahamas. Once out of New York, I set the plane on autopilot and take a nap. Next thing I know, I'm there."

Rex couldn't imagine anything scarier. "I understand you're something of a risk-taker."

Dusk descended early here, without the spectacle of a leisurely Florida sunset, he noted. Brooklyn lit the citronella candle on the patio table.

"I couldn't have gotten where I am today without taking risks. I was born in Brooklyn, but grew up in a trailer in Flint, Michigan. My stepdad worked on the GM assembly line. I painted houses through college. By the time I was twenty-one, I owned my boss's business and my first home—a real brick and mortar one. I bought one house a year after that, rented or flipped them, and then got into investment in a big way."

"Paul Winslow sent me your *curriculum vitae*. It's very impressive."

Brooklyn proffered a disarming piratical smile. "Sorry if I sounded a bit fierce just now. I didn't want you to think I was some kind of playboy with an inherited trust fund."

"Why would I think that?"

His host shrugged expansively. "If Winslow gave you my business credentials, I'm sure he mentioned a few other things as well."

"There was mention of a special closeness between you and Sabine Durand," Rex ventured.

Brooklyn's strong profile turned toward the silhouetted palm trees. "It's true I saw a lot of Sabine. We went horseback riding together. There's a small ranch behind the resort next to the Butterfly Farm. They kept an English saddle for her. She always rode Dancer. I'd take Rocky, the big stallion.

"We went riding most mornings, just the two of us, usually at Galion Beach. We'd remove the saddles and ride into the sea to cool off the horses. I know there was talk. People assumed because we were younger than the rest of the group that something was going on between us, but if there was I would never say anything." He sighed impatiently. "Anyway, it's all nonsense. After our ride that morning, we went our separate ways. I didn't see her again after that."

"When you were with her that morning, did she act as though everything was normal, or did she seem upset?"

"She seemed fine. We talked about going into Marigot that Saturday for the parade. It was her idea originally. We all discussed it at dinner the night before she disappeared, which would have been

July ninth. Sabine, being French, wanted to celebrate the storming of the Bastille. Shame she never lived to enjoy it." Brooklyn's hand tightened into a fist.

"Do you have a photo of her?"

"You've never seen her?"

"I'm not really into the theatre, and if I ever saw a picture of her somewhere, I've forgotten."

Brooklyn got up from his chair and returned with a couple of snapshots. Holding one picture up to the porch light, Rex saw a young woman leaning against the withers of a horse, long copper hair flowing about her shoulders, a secretive smile dimpling her delicate face. Svelte in a white open-necked shirt and jodhpurs, she could have been the advertisement for a lily-based English perfume. Goosebumps crept up his arms, and for a brief moment, he fell under her spell.

"Intoxicating, isn't she?" Brooklyn said.

"Interesting you should describe her that way. I was just thinking of a perfume ad." Rex lifted the second photo to the light. This one showed more of her face—cat-like eyes and chin, a dusting of golden freckles across a finely chiseled nose. Her skin seemed almost translucent, her rosebud mouth a touch petulant.

"I've known a lot of spectacular women," Brooklyn said. "Most of them I've forgotten, but you never forget a woman like Sabine."

Rex reverently handed back the photos. "Aye. It's almost fitting that something mysterious became of her."

"It's mysterious alright," Brooklyn said in a voice gravelly with emotion. "I won't ever rest until I find out what happened out there on the rocks."

THREE

At seven that evening, the Winslows accompanied Rex and Brooklyn to The Cockatoo Restaurant, located just west of the resort. Chinese lanterns swung in the palm trees, lighting their way along the beach. The bay glimmered dark and unfathomable. Ever since Rex could remember, he'd mistrusted water he couldn't see through.

Elizabeth wore a flame-colored pareo knotted at her hip, regal in her bearing, in spite of breasts that were beginning to sag. Her husband had donned a wrap. When they reached the deck of the restaurant, Rex saw that the rest of the clientele was dressed in similar attire. Despite the nude torsos, he decided to keep his shirt on as he could not conceive of sitting down to dinner bare-chested.

"Rex Graves, QC, from Edinburgh," Paul Winslow announced to the group seated at the large outdoor table strewn with an assortment of drinks.

A plump teenage girl fed pistachios to a snowy-white cockatoo perched on the wooden balustrade. "What is QC?" she asked with a light Germanic accent.

"Queen's Counsel. Mr. Graves is a barrister appointed by the Queen of England."

"We're called advocates in Scotland," Rex explained to the girl.

Winslow began introducing the guests. "Age before beauty," he said, putting a hand on the shoulder of a Kirk Douglas look-alike of military bearing. "Vernon Powell."

Rex shook his hand. This was Sabine Durand's husband. Hard to conceive of the delicate beauty wed to this wooden marionette.

"Herr Doktor von Mueller," Winslow then informed him.

"*Nein, nein!*" the bespectacled doctor objected affably. "Max. *Und* may I present my wife Martina *und* daughter Gaby."

The wife and daughter, flaxen-haired and Rubenesque, smiled in fixed beatitude. The von Muellers were not suspects, Rex recalled; they had been in Philipsburg the night of Mademoiselle Durand's disappearance.

"My good friends David and Toni Weeks," Winslow said, continuing the introductions. "Our new chef at Swanmere Manor is a graduate of David's school of French cuisine."

Rex extended his hand, studying the couple whose statements seemed to divulge so much about them. David Weeks, slight in frame like Paul Winslow, and with the legs of a stick insect, had a noticeably weak chin. His wife, Toni, more solidly built, appealed to the eye with her exotic dark looks.

"Duke Farley," boomed a broad-shouldered Texan, without waiting for Winslow to introduce him. "And my wife Pam."

"Enchanted," Rex replied, inclining his head politely at the couple seated at the far side of the table, and attempting not to ogle Pam's breasts, which were the largest he had ever seen while still managing to defy the law of gravity. She reminded him of the full-blown roses he had seen cascading from the walls of a chateau in the Rhône Valley at the peak of their bloom.

"Dick and Penny Irving from Toronto," a bodybuilder said, pursuing the self-introductions.

His wife didn't look like she carried a spare gram of fat either, her arms toned to perfection.

Paul Winslow hastened to make the last introduction. "Sean and Nora O'Sullivan from Dublin, owners of the Coolidge Theatre."

"Pleased to meet you," the elderly man said in a cultivated Irish brogue, his mischievous features reminding Rex of a leprechaun.

"Likewise," his petite, gray-haired wife added. "Come sit down." She indicated a seat by her husband.

The Winslows took the vacant chairs by David and Toni Weeks, while Brooklyn squeezed in next to the teenager Gaby.

"What's everyone drinking?" Paul asked, beckoning a waiter.

"You should try a Hemingway," Weeks told Rex.

"What is that?"

"A magical drink," Sean O'Sullivan chimed in. "Ice-cold coconut water, fresh lime, Gordon's gin, and a dash of bitters."

"I'll try it."

"Good man." The flushed Irishman looked as though he might have had one too many magical drinks already. He draped an arm around the back of Rex's chair. "A sad errand brings you, sure," he lamented. "We'll drink a toast and pray you can solve the mystery of Sabine Durand, God bless her sweet heart."

"I read your sworn statement..." Rex began.

"I had a wee tipple that afternoon, so my memory of events is blurred, I regret to say. But I shall never forget her."

"What was she like?"

"Ah, she was never afraid to try anything. She was Penny's scuba partner, but sometimes we dove together. What was I saying, Nora?" he asked his wife. "Oh, yes. Sabine grew up with horses. The clearest vision I have of her is galloping down the beach, her hair and the horse's mane streaming interchangeably in the breeze. One time we bathed in the sea off the moonlit beach. Ah, Sabine inspired me to write poetry. She was my Maud Gonne."

Nora sighed with impatience. "Just ignore him," she told Rex.

The waiter served his cocktail. Rex took a sip, appreciating the clean taste of the gin, the sharpness of lime, and bite from the Angostura.

"What's the verdict, Counselor?" the Irishman asked, an unlit cigarette wedged in his minuscule mouth.

"Most refreshing."

By and by, the gin began to go to Rex's head, and he was glad when someone mentioned ordering food. A waiter handed him a menu, and Rex opted for a plate of melon and prosciutto, followed by grilled lemon-pepper chicken. Winslow suggested a bottle of Saint-Émilion, but Rex opted for beer.

"Lucky you were able to get away at such short notice," David Weeks addressed him.

"The courts are in summer recess, so it wasna a problem."

"Hope we're not keeping you from your family," Nora O'Sullivan said.

"My son's attending university in Florida, so I took the opportunity of visiting him in Miami on the way here."

"And is there a Mrs. Graves?" the bosomy Pam Farley asked.

"My wife died of cancer five years ago."

Silence chilled the conversation, quickly filled by a few guests voicing their commiserations. Vernon Powell seemed to see Rex for the first time. A glance of sympathy passed between them.

"We must all come here Saturday," Toni Weeks said in a transparent effort to lighten the mood. "Saturday is open mike night at The Cockatoo. It's a lot of fun."

"Is this restaurant owned by the resort?" Rex asked.

"Yes, but it's open to the public, as you can see. The Cockatoo is our usual port of call for dinner. The band starts at eight."

"There's a nightclub called Boo-Boo-Jam at the far end of the beach," drawled the balding, sandy-haired Texan. "Great for kebabs and island music. It's frequented by locals—the air is thick with dope. Sabine caused a sensation. That gal was a very sexy dancer."

Another lull broke the convivial chatter. The waiter appeared to clear away the appetizers. Rex sat back in his chair and contemplated Pam Farley in the wake of her husband's stark compliment. She was younger than Duke, but not young enough to be a trophy wife, though she tried hard to project the illusion. Rex wondered if she had felt threatened by Sabine—if any of the women had.

The closest in age was Penny Irving, another unusually attractive young woman, but whereas the photos portrayed Sabine as fragile and slim almost to the point of anorexia, Penny exuded fitness and health. Winslow had mentioned that she and her husband owned the Body Beautiful chain of health spas across Canada. Rex noticed they had each selected the leanest items on the menu.

He skipped Martina and Gaby von Mueller in his review, since they had an alibi for when Sabine went missing. Nora O'Sullivan, it seemed, had decided to age gracefully and let the gray in her hair show. With her alabaster Irish complexion and cornflower blue eyes, the effect was not unbecoming.

While Elizabeth Winslow recounted an anecdote about her trip to the hairdresser in Marigot that day, Rex took the opportunity to pass the handsome redhead under his scrutiny, guessing her to be in her late forties. Seated beside her, Toni Weeks also retained a noble beauty. According to Paul Winslow, her mother had been a distant relative of the emir of Kuwait and had married an Englishman.

"Our daughters are the same age," Toni told Rex. "Jasmin and Gaby get together each July at La Plage. Jasmin will be here next week. She's spending a fortnight in Nice with her French pen pal."

"*Und* Gaby had Latin school this summer," Martina von Mueller added in heavily accented English. "She arrived a week ago."

"Latin school?" Rex inquired.

"Where we speak Latin," Gaby replied. "I want to study law, so Latin is very important." The girl's English was much better than her mother's.

"Rex is a criminal lawyer, not an entertainment attorney like Vernon," Toni explained to Gaby.

Rex wanted to get back to the subject of Latin school. "*Num Latine ibi cotidie loqueris?*" he asked. Do you speak Latin every day there?

"*Cotidie et omni tempore.*" All day, every day.

"That's amazing. And they say Latin is a dead language."

"So useful to have a background in Latin for medicine also," the Austrian doctor remarked.

"Well, I'd be happy to chat in Latin with you while I'm here," Rex told Gaby, who appeared pleased by the attention.

"So, Rex," Weeks said. "Are you going to be getting into our naturist culture?"

"Och, I dinna know about that," Rex stumbled in his embarrassment, his Scots accent thickening in proportion to the alcohol he drank. "Not much occasion to go about wi' no clothes on back home."

"Is it true that it rains all the time in Scotland?" Brooklyn asked. "I played golf in St. Andrews once and it pissed down every day."

"Aye, just aboot."

"Just like Ireland," Nora said.

"Well, don't be shy, old fellow. We'll let you keep your sporran on."

The table erupted into laughter at David Weeks' comment.

"What's a sporran?" Gaby asked.

"It's a Scottish fanny-pack," said Brooklyn.

The guests laughed uproariously again. The second course arrived, filling the air with an aroma of savory ribs and spicy seafood. Rex attacked his grilled chicken and rice with gusto.

"Grand Case, the neighboring town, is the gastronomic capital of the island," Dick Irving, the Canadian, told him, addressing him for the first time since their introduction. "There are about thirty restaurants packed along the main boulevard."

"I passed by there on the way to the resort."

"You must have taken the Marigot route from the airport," Duke Farley said.

"Aye. The driver was verra informative," Rex added, slipping deeper into his Scots accent. "It was like having my own personal tour guide. Is Pascal the limo driver too?" he asked, remembering the reference to the limousine in Toni Weeks' statement.

"Yeah, but if there's a scheduling conflict, Greg Hastings, the manager, sometimes drives. A few of us rent Jeeps, but cars get broke into so often on the island we prefer to be chauffeured whenever possible."

"Who owns the resort?"

"Monsieur Bijou," Brooklyn replied. "He has another hotel and a new club in Marigot, but lately he's gotten into residential projects. He just opened a luxury condominium complex up the coast."

"Marina del Mar," Paul Winslow said. "He's got fingers in several pies. It's thanks to him the police finally pulled their thumbs out and decided to look into Sabine's disappearance."

"Truth is, we've gotten nowhere in a week," Duke Farley exploded. "She couldn't have just vanished into thin air."

The guests looked expectantly at Rex, who cleared his throat. "Aye, well I'll see what I can do, starting first thing in the morning, but I canna make any promises."

Solving the case of the missing actress might prove to be a challenge. An island in the Caribbean was an ideal place to commit the perfect crime, he reflected. If you could pitch a body far enough into the sea, you could hope the sharks would get to it before the police did. And one week had already gone by.

FOUR

THE NEXT MORNING, REX set out with Paul Winslow for the promontory where Sabine Durand's trail had ended. He was relieved to see that Paul had donned tennis shorts for the expedition. Dick and Penny Irving, the couple from Toronto, were just returning from an early jog along the shore, bodies replete with artful tattoos and rings in their genitals. Their sole items of clothing were matching white sweatbands embroidered in red with "The Body Beautiful."

The presence of such athleticism made Rex momentarily consider liposuction on his love handles. Luckily, the imperfections of his body were concealed in court by a black robe, but he decided then and there to go on a diet.

"Ideal specimens of the human anatomy," Winslow remarked of the Irvings as they ran by. "Puts one to shame, doesn't it?"

"You're in pretty good shape."

"Nowhere near those two, but then I'm too lazy. I suppose they have to be good advertisements for their health spa chain. Vernon works hard at it too. Wouldn't go with the image of an aggressive New York entertainment attorney to be covered in flab."

"Was he in the military?"

"Served in Vietnam, I believe."

"That explains his upright posture and stern demeanor."

"Well, he hasn't much to be happy about with Sabine gone—unless, of course, he had something to do with it. But he never was much of a live wire to begin with."

They approached the boat rental shack, which had not yet opened for the day, and continued past it to the rocky promontory, which rose in their path, gradually sloping into the water.

"Watch yourself on the rocks," Paul warned. "They'll be slippery."

They walked out over the wrinkled wet sand to a low part of the promontory and climbed over to the strip of shore on the other side. Without any wind, there was not enough swell to break on the rocks out at sea.

"Today will be a scorcher," Winslow commented absent-mindedly, staring out to the ocean as though it held the answer to Sabine's disappearance. "I can't bear to think what happened to her."

"I canna understand why she would come out here," Rex said, looking about him. "Especially after dark."

Broken shells and bottles littered the windward part of the island. Scrub grew on the far side, adding to the desolate appearance. A rugged cliff blocked direct access inland, providing a cove hidden from view.

"I always think the water looks forbidding at night," Winslow murmured.

We bathed in the sea off the moonlit beach.

The poetic sound of Sean O'Sullivan's words had taken root in Rex's mind for some reason.

"It's still grey this time of morning," Winslow remarked. "Makes you wonder what's lurking beneath."

"Aye. That's why I don't like the water. I won't go in where I canna see the bottom." Rex scoured the narrow shoreline, but he knew the chances of finding anything of interest were remote. Too many people had traipsed over the sand, not to mention the tide flowing in at regular intervals.

"This is where the gendarmes found her ankle bracelet." Winslow pointed to a spot above the waterline midway along the outcrop of rocks.

"What about the bloody scrap of material?"

"Up there where you're standing. It was caught on a piece of driftwood. The blood matched Sabine's. She had a rare blood type, so there can be no doubt it was hers."

"Who did the testing?"

"Vernon found a lab in Philipsburg. The police wouldn't pay for it. They combed the beach and questioned everyone at the resort, but they refuse to pursue the enquiry until a body is found. They did give us a swatch for the testing, though it took a bit of arm-twisting on our part."

"What did you match the blood with?"

"Max von Mueller performed cosmetic surgery on Sabine five years ago. He called his clinic in Vienna and compared the findings with his records. The blood type was a positive match."

"He's a cosmetic surgeon?"

"One of the best in Europe."

Rex found it surprising that the doctor with the round face and protruding belly was an aesthetic surgeon. He looked more like a psychiatrist or pediatrician.

They headed back toward the resort, where the beach attendants were putting up the yellow umbrellas.

Rex pointed to the island in the mouth of the bay. "What's out there?" he asked Winslow.

"Just piles of shells and a couple of half-sunken wrecks. You can snorkel across."

"What about sharks?"

"Mostly blacknose and reef sharks. A big barracuda may skim the sand alongside you. He's just curious. Barracuda won't bite humans in clear water unless you're wearing something shiny or swimming in a school of fish. Then they might strike by mistake, same as a shark."

Shielding his eyes from the sun, Rex turned to face the direction in which they had come. "What about on the other side, beyond the promontory?"

"I wouldn't go out there unless you're a good swimmer. There's a strong undertow. Looked calm enough this morning, but the waters around the island can get quite rough, which limits visibility for diving."

"Do you dive?"

"Occasionally. Brook's my scuba partner. Penny and Sabine used to pair up. We'd go on shark dives where you feed them and they swim between your legs."

Rex shuddered. "You'd never catch me doing that."

"It does take nerve."

"I worry about my son surfing in Florida."

"Shark attacks are pretty rare," Winslow consoled him, unsuccessfully.

After agreeing to get together later in the day, they diverged in front of the cabanas. As Rex entered his living room through the sliding glass door, Brooklyn was just leaving by the main entrance, dressed in a lightweight suit.

"I left a couple of croissants in the oven for you and some coffee in the pot."

"Thanks. Off to town?"

"I have a meeting in Philipsburg. Catch you later."

Rex took his breakfast to the patio table where the previous day's *Daily Mail* was anchored by a conch shell in case of a sudden gust. Ordinarily, he took exception to the *tsk-tsk* style of the *Daily Mail*, but today he viewed it as a friend from home and eagerly turned to the Sudoku puzzle, which he completed in eight minutes flat. He wished the mystery of the missing actress were as easy to solve.

The full sun on the bay gave the effect of a blue mica mosaic. It looked inviting now, beckoning him for a swim. He prepared for the beach. His concession was to wear a white towel about his waist as though partaking of the Turkish baths. He did not feel comfortable conducting an investigation in his birthday suit, although the public nakedness of others bothered him less than he would have thought.

"The Pillsbury Dough Boy," Duke Farley joked as Rex passed him on the way to the beach. The Texan said it with a pleasant laugh, and Rex didn't take offense.

"You should have seen me before I got to Miami."

Farley, in nothing but flip-flops, clapped him on the shoulder. "Don't forget the sunscreen," he advised. "You don't wanna get fried."

Rex assured him he would do just that and went to find an unclaimed umbrella. The slabs of flesh on the lounge-chairs arranged along the beach reminded him of bodies at a morgue. The women had not gone so far as to discard their jewelry. Mrs. Winslow wore a heavy gold necklace in a Greek key pattern design that must get uncomfortably hot in the sun.

Sabine Durand's ankle bracelet had been found beyond the outcrop of rocks. Rex pondered the significance of that. The blood on the torn strip of pareo, discovered in the same location, had proved to belong to her too. Something had happened out there. But what?

The absence of a body was not necessarily a bar to a murder charge, at least not in English law. St. Martin, part of the Department of Guadeloupe, was subject to French law. What he needed to ascertain was whether Sabine Durand had been murdered and who had killed her. The French authorities could take it from there.

Spotting a vacant lounge-chair next to Pam Farley, he asked if he might ask a few questions.

Pam flashed him a toothy smile. "Go right ahead," she said in a welcoming Southern twang. Winslow had told him not to be taken in by her dazzling blonde looks. She had graduated *magna cum laude* from an Ivy League college and been clever enough to snag an oil and cattle tycoon.

Rex perched on the chair. "Your statement pretty much fits with the others. What I wanted to ask you was about Sabine herself."

"What about her?" Pam settled more comfortably on her saffron-colored towel.

Like the other women he had seen *au naturel*, she was shaved to within an inch of her life. He concentrated instead on the attractively proportioned features of her face.

"Your personal recollections, how she behaved the last time you saw her, that sort of thing."

"The last time I saw her was a week ago Tuesday at Happy Hour. We were at l'Apéritif, that tiki bar over there. It must have been around eleven a.m. We were drinking piña coladas—the usual crowd, except for the Irvings who had gone to St. Barts for the day. There's not much to see on that island, so we declined their invitation to join them. After drinks, the von Muellers went to pick up their daughter from the airport and stayed on the Dutch side for dinner. Sabine, Toni, Nora, and Elizabeth went into Philipsburg for lunch. I had booked a session at the resort spa at three so I didn't go with them."

"And then?"

"After my massage and facial, I stayed in my cabana to wash and set my hair, and didn't see my friends, all but Sabine, until dinner. I can't remember exactly what time Duke got back from his dive, but he was already showered and changed when I was through getting ready."

"How did Sabine seem that day?"

"Much the same as usual. I mean, when you talked to her, you always wondered if she was listening to a word you said. Her aquamarine eyes would just drift away and then, just when you thought you'd lost her, she would smile vaguely and say something apt." She waved to a bronzed couple at the water's edge.

"So, you weren't exactly close?" Rex prompted, drawing her attention back to him.

She inspected her immaculate manicure. "This is the third year I've been coming to the Plage d'Azur and I can't say I ever figured her out. Sabine was private about her past life. I believe she came from a well-to-do family of bankers in Paris, but fell out with her mother and had not seen her father in years. In any case, that's what she told me. I think she was close to her father, and that may explain her air of tragedy. Unless that too was an act."

"What do you mean by that?"

"I thought her a bit of an actress, even outside of work. She was my least favorite woman friend of the group, to tell the truth—which, of course, I'm duty bound to do." Pam beamed him another brilliant smile. "You are, after all, investigating her disappearance in a semi-official capacity. Still," she added, "I couldn't help but admire her, just as you would have to admire a Lalique statuette."

It was becoming apparent to Rex that Sabine did not have many fans among the female guests. He wondered what other reactions he might receive. Across the beach he could make out a tall form reclining on a lounge chair beneath an umbrella, a bejeweled right hand clasping a tall drink, the straw hat bobbing as the owner chatted to a neighbor.

"Is that Elizabeth Winslow?"

Pam squinted. "Yes. She's talking to Nora."

"I'll go and bother them now. Your husband will be wanting his chair."

"Duke went to play racquet ball with Vernon. They play every morning. As the oldest men in the group they have to work harder at staying in shape."

"You all look so fit. I'm beginning to get a complex."

"You look just fine to me for a man your size," Pam complimented him with a seductive smile.

Covering his embarrassment with a polite cough, Rex took his leave of the Southern belle and, adjusting the towel around his waist, made his way to Mrs. Winslow's spot, greeting several guests on the way.

The night before, he had asked them to confine themselves to the resort for the next few days for interviews and, for the most part, they had complied with civility, expressing themselves anxious to find out who had committed the crime. Brooklyn had pleaded business appointments, but had promised to make himself available whenever possible. None had provable alibis other than the von Muellers and possibly the Irvings, whose itineraries he would have to verify.

According to David Weeks' testimony, Sabine was last seen just after six p.m., which was close to the time when the male members of the group returned from their diving excursion. No one began looking for Sabine until ten that night. A window of four hours existed during which time she vanished. If a guest had killed her, there was only one hour of opportunity before they all met up at The Cockatoo restaurant for Paul Winslow's birthday dinner at seven.

Rex hoped that under constant surveillance the perpetrator might give himself or herself away by making that incriminating slip that everyone did sooner or later. Possible, too, that the body might be washed ashore during that time. Or what was left of it.

FIVE

"Good morning," Elizabeth Winslow greeted Rex behind a huge pair of designer sunglasses. "Are you going to try to cultivate a tan?"

"I canna spend ten minutes in the sun without turning pink."

"Nor can I with my Irish complexion," Nora said from the lounge-chair beside Elizabeth's.

"I was a sun-worshipper when I was younger," Elizabeth confided. "Now I'm paying for it." She had the fragile skin of a natural redhead. In broad daylight, the heavy gold jewelry around her neck could not hide the sun spots and premature wrinkling on her chest. "Won't you have a drink?" she asked. "The waiter will be along in a minute."

"It's still a bit early for me."

"Oh, we don't have rules here," Elizabeth said in her well-bred English voice. "Besides, alcohol is so cheap out here it's criminal not to take advantage."

Nora relinquished her spot beside Elizabeth. "I'm going to do my laps. Rex, you're welcome to use my chair for twenty minutes."

He duly slipped into the lounger beneath the shade of the umbrella. A parade of nudists strolled along the beach while couples and families frolicked in the sea. If his starchy Scottish colleagues could only see him now ...

"So," Elizabeth began. "We dragged you halfway across the Caribbean to look into our friend's disappearance. What do you think now that you're here?"

"It's a bit soon to say."

"Forgive my impatience. You only arrived yesterday afternoon, after all."

"I take it you were close to Sabine Durand?"

"We met ten years ago when she came from Paris to work at David's restaurant. That was before he opened his cookery school. David and Toni had a small flat in Kensington back then, so Sabine lodged with us. Paul and I became quite attached to her. We married late and have no children of our own."

"And you've kept in contact with her ever since."

"We didn't see so much of her when she became involved in the theatre. The hours of rehearsal were grueling and she toured a lot. But she dropped us a line here and there, and I saved all the programmes and newspaper articles for my scrapbook."

"What do you, personally, think became of her, Mrs. Winslow?"

"Elizabeth—please." She removed her sunglasses, revealing green eyes glassy with tears. "It's not easy to say this," she said. "But I'm going to anyway. I'm certain her husband is involved. When I heard she was going to marry a much older man, I was, to say the least, concerned. Sabine was such a romantic creature. I couldn't see what attraction she could feel for a hardnosed New York law-yer, however rich he might be. But I suppose she felt he could further her career. She was doing a stint on Broadway when they met."

Rex privately acknowledged that the husband was the most logical suspect. His cell phone had been found by the rocks. Paul Winslow had pointed the finger at Vernon too, citing his jealousy, but without concrete evidence, murder would be hard to prove.

"Have you seen the police report?" Elizabeth asked.

"Not yet. I only know what your husband told me and what I read in the statements faxed to me in Edinburgh. Did Sabine ever discuss her marriage with you?"

Elizabeth nodded, studying the sunglasses in her hand. "About a week ago I noticed a nasty bruise on her arm and when I asked her about it, she laughed it off saying she'd fallen from a horse. I must have looked skeptical because after a while her eyes sort of misted up, and she told me she had fought with Vernon and that he'd grabbed her arm in a rage."

"Did she say what they were fighting about?"

"No, but I suspect it was over Brooklyn Chalmers." Elizabeth put her sunglasses back on. "Sabine never admitted to it but, if you ask me, they were much more suited to one another. Brooklyn has youth and vitality, a passion for life. Vernon is so … wooden."

Rex knew he would have to elicit precise details from Vernon Powell as to his whereabouts at the time his wife vanished. He felt his heart hardening against the man. Rex couldn't abide the idea of violence against women, and Sabine seemed such a delicate creature, quite incapable of defending herself.

He watched Nora O'Sullivan perform a vigorous crawl back to shore and then wade out of the water, shaking her short gray hair like a wet dog. Rex got up and handed her the fluffy yellow towel as she approached.

"Ah, I feel fine after my swim. You should go in, Elizabeth."

"I think I will." Elizabeth took an inflatable raft with her.

Nora spread her towel across her friend's lounge chair and lay down. "I suppose you'll be wanting to question me now."

"Only if it's convenient," Rex said, sitting back down.

"Ask away. I have nothing to hide. I didn't want to talk in front of Elizabeth because she was fond of the girl. You may find my impressions rather different."

"Well, let's start with what you wrote in your statement. You went with Elizabeth, Sabine, and Toni Weeks to Philipsburg last Tuesday and didn't see Sabine again after you all arrived back at the resort at about four-thirty, is that right?"

"It is. The last I saw of her was when she was getting out of the limo. She said she was going to reception to check her messages, and I said I'd see her later at Paul's birthday dinner. When Sean and I got to the restaurant, everyone was there except her."

"Vernon was there too?"

"No, I was forgetting. He arrived after us. He said he'd waited for his wife at their cabana until the last moment and then decided she must have gone straight to The Cockatoo from her walk."

"What was his reaction when he saw she wasn't at the restaurant?"

"He seemed calm enough, maybe a bit icy—as though he might be cross that she was late for Paul's party."

"And your husband was with you since what time?"

"Sixish. I was in the bath, but I heard him come in. The men had been scuba diving."

"Did Sabine seem in good spirits when you were in Philipsburg?"

"That she did. She seemed exited about the upcoming parade in Marigot. Of course, had she been alive during the Storming of the Bastille, she would hardly have been on the side of the peasants. But Sabine had her whims and we all thought it was a charming idea."

"Did she mention whether she was expecting news of any kind when she left to pick up her messages?"

"I don't think so. As you know, the cabanas don't have phones, so it's quite usual for guests to go to the main building to see if anyone's tried to make contact."

"Why don't the cabanas have phones?"

"It's considered obtrusive. And I must say, I don't miss having one when I'm here."

Rex mentally added a visit to reception to his list of things to do. Perhaps someone had left a message for a rendezvous with Sabine. "What if an urgent message came through?" he asked Nora. "How would it reach you?"

"A member of the staff would deliver a note. That's what happened with the von Muellers. Gaby missed her connection and called the resort to let her parents know she'd be on a later flight." Nora rummaged in her beach bag and drew out a comb. "Any messages to do with Sabine's acting work go to Vernon, since he acts as her manager." She said this with some vexation.

"You don't approve?"

"Ah, well, it's water under the bridge now, but a few years ago Sabine was supposed to play the lead role at our theatre in Dublin. When she was offered a part in a Broadway production, Vernon finagled her out of her contract with us, and the play went bust. We couldn't get another crowd-drawing actress to fill the role in time. Sabine was ambitious. She'd been trying to get into film. She felt the lure of Hollywood and no doubt thought exposure on Broadway would help."

"Was she extremely talented?"

"She had stage presence," Nora conceded. "How that would have translated onto screen, I can't tell you. I suppose, at twenty-eight, she decided it was now or never. You can cover a multitude of sins under stage makeup and lighting, but the camera isn't so forgiving. She probably thought she could always return to the stage later."

"And your impressions of Sabine Durand as a person?" Rex asked as Nora applied suntan lotion to her face with the aid of a tortoiseshell compact similar to the one described in Toni Weeks' statement.

"She was straight out of Daphne du Maurier's *Rebecca*. In fact, it would not surprise me if Sabine did style herself after some literary character. She was not your typical flesh-and-blood woman. I'd be very surprised if a shark would bother to go after her as the police seem to think. She was very will-o'-the-wisp."

"What do you think happened to her?"

Nora shrugged. "She knew a lot of men. Any one of them could have killed her out of jealousy."

Rex watched as she dropped the compact back in her beach bag. "Did you get that item here?" he asked. "I'd like to get one for a friend."

"In Philipsburg. I'll try and remember which shop and let you know."

At that moment, Elizabeth returned with her raft. "Hope I didn't come back too soon," she said looking from one to the other as she patted herself down with her yellow resort towel.

Rex gave up his seat. "Your timing is perfect. I have a few errands to run."

"I was thinking," Elizabeth said. "If you're still here at the end of the month, there's a Full Moon Party in Grand Case on the thirtieth. You can see the stars for miles around."

"'Tis true enough," Nora chirped in. "There's no better place for stargazing than in the Caribbean, away from all the artificial light and pollution of big cities."

Rex told them he would attend if he could, though he secretly wished Moira Wilcox could be there with him. Stargazing was not an activity meant for one. He wondered what the night skies looked like in war-torn Baghdad, where his girlfriend was involved in humanitarian work restoring schools and bringing mobile water purification plants to the residents. In May, five British nationals had been abducted from a government building in the center of the city. He had not heard from Moira in two months. Fearing she had been kidnapped by terrorists, he had contacted the British Embassy in Baghdad before leaving on his trip, requesting assistance in ascertaining her whereabouts.

Securing the towel about his middle, he thanked the two women for their time and made his way to the main building, a larger chalet than the eight beach residences, with steps leading up to the wooden porch.

"Anything for Rex Graves?" he asked at the desk. His mother was under strict instructions to call if news came from Baghdad.

The female clerk searched in the first pigeonhole and handed him a postcard of an orange sunset bleeding into the ocean, postmarked Puerto Rico. It was from Helen d'Arcy, whom he had met over Christmas at Swanmere Manor in Sussex, since which time they had kept loosely in contact. Conscious of the smile stretching his lips, he read the few lines.

> *Wish you were here! I went ahead and booked my passage on the Sun-Fun Cruise Line. Will dock at St. Martin on July 23rd. Meet me off the* Olympia *at 11 for lunch? Love, Helen*

How the devil was he supposed to contact her at sea? With difficulty. But that was the point, he supposed; she was giving him little choice. He had been noncommittal about her proposed visit to St. Martin when she suggested it. Not that he didn't want to see her—he did—he just felt conflicted by the situation with Moira.

All the same, he couldn't prevent Helen from spending her summer wherever she chose, and clearly she wanted to spend part of it with him. He wondered if he would be able to resist her this time in such an idyllic and seductive setting.

"I don't suppose my suitcase arrived?"

The young desk clerk shook her head in apology. "*Désolée*. Anything else I can help you with?"

"Perhaps … Did you happen to be on duty last Tuesday afternoon?"

She nodded.

"I wonder if you remember Ms. Durand coming in and asking for her messages?"

The clerk frowned in concentration. "I think so, yes. Do you know what happened to her? It is terrible!"

"I don't know anything at present. I was hoping you might help me. I'm assisting the gendarmes in their investigation." This was a stretch, since he had not yet formally made his acquaintance with the police—an oversight he aimed to rectify immediately after lunch.

"Generally she received many letters, and occasionally phone messages from a chiropractor's office." The clerk turned to the mailbox for #2 and extracted a few items. "Monsieur Powell has been picking up the mail."

"I'm heading back that way. I can take those." Rex held out his hand, brooking no protest.

As he left the lobby, he flipped through the envelopes and messages. One message, dated just over a week ago, was marked for Sabine's attention. It was from a Dr. Sganarelle's office confirming an appointment.

Vernon Powell did not answer when he knocked. At Brook's cabana, Rex changed into his one set of spare clothes and went to find Paul Winslow.

"I'm going to join my wife for lunch at The Cockatoo. Why don't you join us?"

"Actually, I'm off to the Gendarmerie in Grand Case and wondered if I could borrow your Jeep."

"Of course, dear man. Just remember they drive on the wrong side of the road here. And don't leave anything inside the car as it

46

may get vandalized." Winslow threw him the keys, and Rex took off for the neighboring town.

Turning out of the resort, he maneuvered around the potholes that heavy rains had gutted into craters and gullies. He couldn't imagine why this long dirt stretch wasn't better maintained by the resort and by the ranch and butterfly farm that it serviced. No wonder the guests rented Jeeps.

Once on the main road, another hazard awaited: bleating goats—zillions of them. He slowed to a stop while they plodded across the asphalt to the grassy hills on the other side. Cars began forming a long line behind him before he was finally able to move again.

The coast road that circled into Grand Case gave a bird's-eye view of the tiki bars and souvenir huts along the Plage d'Azur. A couple of windsurfers skated in zigzag patterns across the bay. A small sailboat made for the island, gliding through the blue waves.

Passing a large salt pond, he turned into a street bisecting the main boulevard of the town and found a parking space in front of one of many restaurants by the beach. He selected a bistro from where he could watch over Winslow's Jeep, and ordered a coffee and a toasted ham and cheese sandwich.

"Oooh ay le commissariat?" he asked the waiter when he had finished lunch, his guttural Scots tongue never having mastered the nuances of French pronunciation.

"*Par là-bas*," the man said pointing down the street. "*Rue de Hollande*."

Rex decided to walk to the police station since there were limited opportunities for parking. Beyond the stop sign at the intersection, a two-story building displayed the French tricolor flag, the words "GENDARMERIE" painted across its pitted façade. He mounted the steps and found the door locked. A glance at his watch confirmed it was past the hour for even an extended French lunch. Perhaps the police took naps, he thought crossly.

As he turned away, a gendarme exited a house on the other side of the street, straightening his blue uniform.

"Poovee-voo m'aider?" Rex gamely asked as the man approached. He was almost as tall as Rex, but thin as a beanpole.

"*Bien-sûr. Lieutenant Pierre Latour à votre service.*" The gendarme gave a slight bow.

In spite of the officer's assurances of help, Rex could swear he detected a smirk on his face. "Je suis Monsieur Graves. Parlez-voo anglez?"

"*Oh, moi, l'anglais, vous savez... Alors*, euh, what, er, is passing?" Apparently, Latour's English was no better than Rex's French.

"I have come about Sabine Durand's disappearance."

The gendarme twiddled his mustache. "We come and search ze beach, ask many questions." A Gallic shrug of the shoulders.

"I am aware of all that. I wondered if I might see the report."

"And your, euh, connection with ze case?"

"I am here at the request of Monsieur Bijou."

Upon mention of the magical name, the officer snapped to attention. "We look all over ze island," he insisted. "We go to ze hotels and make sure ze young lady has not boarded a plane or a ferry." He held out his hands as if to indicate there was nothing else to be done. "But come. I show you ze report."

Unlocking the front door of the station house, he led Rex into a feebly lit lobby and asked him to wait while a copy of the report was made. A few minutes later, Latour returned with two typed sheets stapled together. As Rex scanned the report, he came across several French words he did not recognize.

"*Requins*?" he asked.

The officer formed an upright triangle with his hands and slowly slid them sideways, humming the ominous theme from *Jaws*.

"Sharks?"

Latour nodded. "*Ah, oui, monsieur. Évidemment.*"

"Merci," Rex said. "I'll call if I have any questions."

As he turned to leave, the gendarme wished him *bonne chance*.

"How did it go?" Paul Winslow asked when Rex dropped off the Jeep.

"I met with Lieutenant Latour. He wasna verra cooperative."

"I didn't expect he would be. That's why we sent for you. We were getting nowhere."

Rex waved the papers in his hand. "I did get a copy of the missing person's report. It's in French."

"Elizabeth can help you with that. She lived in Paris for a number of years as a student."

"From what I gather, the police are blaming sharks."

"Well, it's the most facile explanation and absolves them from having to get off their froggy *derrières* and do something about it."

"They did send out a plane, apparently." Rex had noticed the word *avion* on the report.

"It was probably a training exercise the navy has to perform at regular intervals." Winslow clapped him on his sunburned back, and Rex winced. "We're relying on you, old chap. What next?"

"I'd like to talk to the Austrian doctor."

"He's on the beach with his wife and daughter."

When Rex returned to his cabana to change, he was ecstatic to see his suitcase waiting inside the door. He undressed and pulled on his Bermuda trunks, purchased in Miami. Then, sunscreen, notepad and pen in hand, he headed toward the beach where he easily spotted the rotund von Mueller family.

"*Guten Tag*," greeted the bespectacled doctor.

The blonde wife and daughter smiled at Rex before wading into the shallows hand in hand.

"Can I have a quick word?"

"*Natürlich.*" The doctor gestured for him to sit down on one of a trio of lounge-chairs draped with yellow towels. "Please, proceed with your questions."

"Thank you. First of all, I understand you have known Sabine for five years."

"*Ja*. First in a professional capacity. Then we met again here on St. Martin. I never forget a face I have worked on!"

"Did you do much work on her face?" Rex doubted science could fashion a face so naturally perfect as hers.

"*Nein, nein.*" The doctor gave a dismissive wave of the hand. "A little bump on her nose—I remove it. A simple procedure. *Und* I erase a scar on her temple from a riding accident in Fontainebleau when she was a child. Other than the rhinoplasty, there was not much room for improvement. Her bone structure was *perfekt!*"

"Paul told me you were able to match the blood found on the beach with Ms. Durand's blood type on file at your clinic."

"That too was easy. Sabine had a very rare blood type."

"How rare?"

"Type A Kp(b-)."

It sounded like his son's American fraternity house, and Rex's puzzlement must have shown.

"Other than the major ABO blood groups, there are more than two hundred minor groups," the jovial doctor explained. "About one in a thousand people inherit a rare type, *und* this particular type is extremely rare and belongs only to Caucasians."

"So there can be little doubt it was hers?"

Von Mueller resolutely shook his head.

"Doctor, in your professional opinion, did Ms. Durand seem like someone who might have drowned herself?"

"*Nein und abermals nein!* A thousand times no! Sabine had so much to live for."

"Have you any idea what might have happened out there?" Rex gazed pensively toward the promontory.

The doctor lifted his round pink shoulders in a gesture of despair. "Perhaps she smashed her head on a rock? But no. Her body would have been found if she was that close to shore. There was no trace of sea water on the strip of material, so it could not have been washed ashore. *Und* there was so little blood—unless the rest was washed away. It is possible she was dragged to the water."

Rex recognized the validity of the doctor's statement. Short of burying the body in the sand, there was nowhere else to dispose of it. A sheer cliff at the back of the promontory cut off the beach, and the barrier of jagged rocks would have made it difficult to carry a body across without being seen, since the resort stood barely a mile away. At nighttime, such a feat would have been almost impossible.

"She might have been strangled," Rex hypothesized. "Barehanded or with the rest of the pareo. That would account for there not being more blood at the spot where the material was found. If that's the case, her attacker is less likely to be a woman, unless she's verra strong."

"There could have been some sort of struggle," the doctor agreed. "Her broken ankle bracelet was found closer to the water. Anything might have happened there."

"We don't have much to go on." Rex glanced at the doctor in the adjacent lounge-chair. "What time did your daughter's flight get in last Tuesday?"

"Five o'clock. Then we went to The Créole House in Philipsburg for dinner. Gaby was hungry. She says she never gets enough to eat on the plane."

Gaby could afford to miss a meal, Rex thought uncharitably; not that he could talk. He surveyed the spare tire bulging over the waist of his Bermudas and resolved to lose it by the end of his trip. Salad, grilled meat and fish, he promised himself. No beer.

"We returned to our cabana at eight-fifteen or so. We didn't go out again," von Mueller added, answering Rex's next question. "We helped Gaby unpack *und* then we all went to bed."

That left Vernon Powell, Paul Winslow, David Weeks, Sean O'Sullivan, and Duke Farley of the male guests, who had all gone diving on July 10.

A telephone conversation with the captain of the *Ocean Explorer* later that afternoon confirmed that the dive boat had dropped the men off down the beach by the village just before six, although only Toni Weeks had been able to pinpoint the time of her husband's arrival: 6:00 p.m. The other wives had been in their bathrooms preparing for Paul's party. Dick and Penny Irving, who had been on a day excursion to St. Barts, had missed the dinner at The Cockatoo, as had the von Muellers.

As Rex returned to the beach from the main building, he wondered if anything further might be gleaned from the police report. He would ask Mrs. Winslow to translate it. He saw her, cocktail in hand, in the spot she had occupied that morning, contemplating the cover of *People Magazine*, which featured a photograph of Sabine Durand's unforgettable face along with the caption, "Into Thin Air."

SIX

HALF AN HOUR BEFORE sunset, Rex went back to the promontory he had visited that morning with Paul Winslow. Nine days before, Weeks had seen Ms. Durand heading toward this point at just after six, giving her ample time to return before it grew dark.

The Weeks, strolling toward the resort, stopped when they drew level with him.

"Are you going to the crime scene?" Toni asked.

"I wanted to get a feel for the place when it's dark."

"Night falls like a curtain out here. Don't get stranded."

"I brought a flashlight."

"We'll see you back at the resort," David said. "Swing by for a drink at The Cockatoo."

"Will do." Rex, impatient to be on his way, walked on toward the outline of rocks before him.

Standing on the most prominent boulder, he surveyed the darkening expanse of sea. He imagined Sabine standing there as he now was, her white pareo billowing in the breeze. What had she been thinking in those last few moments? Was someone waiting for her behind the rocks? Was it someone she knew? Is that why she hadn't screamed? If she had, someone might have heard. Any footprints would have been washed over by the tide or else trampled before the police got there.

David Weeks' cabana stood at the near end of the row. He was the only person to have seen her on her walk, but anyone who knew her routine could have hidden on the beach until she arrived. There had been a quarter moon that night, according to several statements. At around ten o'clock, the security guards had flashed their lights over the beach looking for a body, but it was not until the next morning when the gendarmes searched the area that the ankle bracelet and scrap of pareo were found. These were the last physical traces of her. The caption from *People Magazine* played through his mind: *Into Thin Air*.

"Where are you, Sabine?" he asked the darkness.

Silence echoed from the looming cliffs and empty sea, followed by the mocking cry of seagulls. Clambering back down the rocks, he turned toward the resort, consoled by the prospect of a cold beer. Just one, he assured himself, recalling his resolution to drop a few extra pounds.

At The Cockatoo, he found most of the resort guests in their pareos and wraps gathered at one end of the bar. Sean O'Sullivan sat by himself, staring into the bottom of his tumbler. "*Me oul shagogsha*," he said when he saw Rex.

Rex took the stool beside him and ordered a Guinness.

"A man of taste," the Irishman approved. His hands shook as he touched his lighter to his cigarette.

A white-shirted bartender gave him the evil eye, even though the restaurant was open to the outdoors on two sides and no one was dining yet.

"You saw Latour from the Gendarmerie today," O'Sullivan said, studiously ignoring the bartender.

"News travels fast."

"That it does. And I suppose you're none the wiser for your visit."

"What makes you say that?"

"This whole investigation is a load of cock. They know full well what happened to Sabine, but they're not saying."

"Who is 'they'?"

"The gendarmes, the whole lot o' them."

"What do they know?"

The Irishman touched his nose. "Ask that cute-hoor Bijou."

"I'm seeing him tomorrow. What can you tell me?"

O'Sullivan cast a conspiratorial look about him. "There's been a string of missing women. All beautiful, all white."

"I'm listening."

"He's sponsored various recreational projects on the island: kiddie playgrounds, botanical parks, golf courses. His luxury residential project is doing a lot to enhance the French side, boosting the economy and attracting a posh class of tourist. He pretty much has the authorities in his pocket. He's as good as royalty here, that he is."

"What has this to do with missing women?"

"I heard he started out with seedy strip clubs in Amsterdam, and that he may have run prostitution rings before that. Girls were found tortured to death. They were all linked to his name, one way or t'other." O'Sullivan signaled to the bartender for another drink and laid two fingers on his glass.

The bartender poured a double shot of whiskey. Rex thought it just as well the Irishman didn't have to get behind the wheel afterward; all he need do was stumble to the sixth cabana down the beach.

"Rumour has it his name isn't really Bijou," he continued as the bartender moved away to serve another customer. "*Bijou* is just a nickname—'Jewel' in French. The murders in Amsterdam were called the Jewel Killings because semi-precious stones were found in the dead girls' mutilated navels. His real name is Coenraad van Bijhooven. About two years ago, a girl was found bound and gagged in a cellar on St. Martin, dead for over a week. A ruby was embedded where her bellybutton should have been. Now, I ask you, is that not a striking coincidence?"

"Was anyone arrested?"

"Some vagrants were brought in for questioning, for form's sake. Unlikely any of them would have left a ruby behind, d'you think?" O'Sullivan blew a puff of cigarette smoke into the ceiling, where a cockatoo preened its feathers on a trapeze.

"Did Bijou's name come up?"

"One rag on the island dug up some dirt and rehashed the Amsterdam murders. Our Mr. Bijou sued the pants off them. Never another word was mentioned."

"Why would a man like Bijou resort to torture and murder?"

"He's a vicious, hedonistic shite, that's why."

"You've met him?"

"Once was enough. His eyes are as cold as the concrete he entombs the girls in."

"Someone could be trying to frame him." Or else the story was all hooey, a fantastical figment of the Irishman's imagination.

O'Sullivan sagged in his chair. "Sure," he said, dispiritedly gazing into his whiskey. *Where are you, Sabine?* Rex imagined him asking the dregs, just as he himself had addressed the darkness just minutes ago.

After a prolonged silence, he decided to leave Sean O'Sullivan to his drink-induced demons. Squeezing him on the shoulder, he got up off his stool. "Catch you later," he said.

"Tooraloo."

Rex joined the rest of the group, who were discussing Vernon Powell. Sabine's husband, it seemed, was keeping to his cabana and not answering the door. According to Paul Winslow, who lived next door, maid service had been unable to get in. "If he doesn't surface tomorrow," he announced, "we had better get management to open up."

"I don't think we need worry that he topped himself," David Weeks said. "When we passed his cabana on our way here, we heard Broadway hits playing at top volume."

"We should leave him be," Toni advised. "Let him work it out of his system."

"Work what out of his system?" Elizabeth Winslow demanded. "We don't know if he's grieving or gloating."

"Really, Elizabeth," her husband chided.

"Don't be a hypocrite," she returned. "You know he did it."

Rex thought he should try to diffuse the situation. "I'll go and see Vernon tomorrow."

"About time," Duke Farley muttered. "He's the one with all the answers."

"Why d'you say that?" Rex asked.

"It's obvious he knows more than he's letting on," the Texan responded belligerently. "That's why he's avoiding us."

"Brooklyn Chalmers isn't around much either," Rex pointed out. "And I don't think he's got anything to hide."

"I wouldn't be so sure," Dick Irving said, looking like Tarzan in his short wrap. "He and Sabine were tight."

"Pretty lady!" a voice chirped.

Rex glanced up toward the rafters where a yellow-breasted macaw wrapped its claws around a second trapeze, trailing blue tail feathers.

"This place is a veritable aviary," Rex commented. "How many birds are there here?"

Penny Irving threw it a cashew, which the macaw adroitly caught in its hooked beak. "Four, all in the parrot family. This is Long John. He was Sabine's favorite."

"Pretty lady!"

"He says that every time he hears her name."

"He misses her," Winslow said. "O'Sullivan's already in his cups, I see," he murmured to Rex, with a sideways look down the bar. "What was he rambling on about?"

"He seems to have a conspiracy theory regarding Ms. Durand's disappearance."

"Don't tell me. Monsieur Bijou is a sadistic serial rapist, but the police are too cowardly to do anything about it."

"In a nutshell."

"Poor old sod. His mind's shot. He has the shakes, you know. Suffers from cirrhosis of the liver."

"Why is he still drinking?"

"Can't quit. Nora put him in rehab but he managed to sneak out to the local pub. He's incorrigible."

Rex chuckled. "An incorrigible Irishman. Fancy that. So there's no truth to this story of his?"

"What do you think?"

"It's verra far-fetched," Rex conceded. "All the same, I'll have my colleague in London do a background check on Mr. Bijou—see what comes up. What can you tell me about him?"

"He's very respected on the island. He's given the French side a certain *caché* it never had before. His private marina community is attracting big money. And he's creating a night life to rival the Dutch side."

"Strip clubs?"

"My dear man!" Winslow clapped him on the shoulder. "Nothing so sleazy. Tasteful nudity—artistic stuff. You really must meet him."

"I intend to. What's his nationality?"

Winslow looked puzzled. "I really can't say. He speaks perfect English and French, but now you mention it, I don't think he's either. You'll find him very cosmopolitan. Remind me to give you his number later. He's not an easy man to pin down."

"The island's not that big."

"Twenty-one square miles on the French side, sixteen on the Dutch," Winslow informed him.

"What's your poison?" the Texan asked Rex.

"Guinness—thanks." One more only, just to be sociable.

"A Guinness over here," Duke Farley boomed across the bar. "Didn't mean to sound off about Vernon earlier," he told Rex. "I just want to put a lid on this business and get on with my vacation.

If Vernon killed the gal, he needs to fess up and get it off his chest—give the rest of us a break."

"I appreciate your sentiments," Rex said. "But he's not the only suspect."

"Did you read my statement?"

"Of course."

"I never was much good at writing essays. That's why I went into oil and cattle. 'But here goes nothing,' I thought at the time. I felt I should describe that scene at our ranch when Vernon and Sabine came to visit last year. Things got pretty ugly."

"So I read."

In his statement, Duke had gone into detail about an argument between the couple over a young stable hand at his Silver Springs Ranch in Texas. The upshot was Vernon had slapped Sabine across the face, leaving an ugly welt that prevented her from making public appearances for two weeks.

Rex almost smiled when he thought about the effort the police must have gone to in order to have the pages of Duke Farley's statement translated, written as they were in Texan vernacular—if in fact they had been translated. Judging by Rex's earlier meeting with Lieutenant Latour, it was highly doubtful the Gendarmerie had gone to the trouble of making certified translations.

"Ah, here comes my lovely wife," Duke exclaimed.

Pam, her chest visibly preceding her, sashayed over to the bar in a gold pareo spangled with silver hibiscus flowers.

"What you drinking, honey? I was just talking to Rex about the time Vernon and Sabine came to stay at the ranch."

"Highly embarrassing for everybody," Pam told Rex. "Sabine had her face on ice for two days. Fortunately, the paparazzi didn't know she was at Silver Springs, so news of the fight never got out. Our staff is very discrete and our nearest neighbors live five miles away. We had to turn down invitations and tell people Sabine had come down with an ear infection."

"What happened about the stable boy?" Rex asked.

"Jason? Why, nothing," Pam replied. "He wasn't to blame. He just happens to be real cute, and caught Sabine's eye. He was saddling her horse one morning, and they were laughing and maybe flirting just a little, but it got on Vernon's last nerve. He dragged her inside the house and backhanded her. I could hear the blow clear across the hall. When I got to her, she was clinging to the newel post. Not crying—I guess the shock was too great at that point. Vernon, well, he just stared, like he couldn't believe what he'd done. As soon as he saw me, he marched off out the door, muttering, 'She darn well asked for it.'"

"Then Pam called me," Duke growled, "thinking he might go after Jason. I told the boy to lay low for the rest of their visit."

"I felt bad for Sabine, but she really brought it upon herself. You don't wave a red flag at a bull."

"That gal had spirit alright!" Duke drawled in admiration. "She was more woman than most guys could handle."

Pam's baby blue eyes blazed her husband with a contemptuous look. Rex thought she was probably more woman than most husbands could wish for, but then some men never were satisfied. The night had lost its glamour, the guests looked jaded, tensions ran high. Even the band sounded flat. Rex decided to call it a night and make a fresh start on the case in the morning.

SEVEN

Bright and early the next morning, Rex made his way to the main building, hoping for news from home. It was too soon for a letter from Iraq to have been forwarded to the Caribbean, but his mother would call him at the resort if any word came from Moira or from the British Embassy. He experienced a twinge of guilt when he thought about Helen arriving in a few days.

Och, she's just a friend, he told himself; and Paul Winslow had told him to enjoy himself while he was here.

"Nothing for you today, monsieur," said the front desk clerk who had been on duty the previous day and whose name, he had discovered, was Danielle.

"Do you have the times of ferries to St. Barts departing from Oyster Pond?"

She handed him a schedule. The ferry left for St. Barts, twenty kilometers away, at nine in the morning, returning from Gustavia Harbor at 5:00 p.m. and docking back at St. Martin approximately forty-five minutes later.

"How long is the drive to Oyster Pond?"

"No more than thirty minutes."

That would get the Irvings back to the resort at around 6:20, factoring in disembarkation, and yet, they had not joined the other guests at The Cockatoo at seven o'clock. "May I use your phone?" he asked the desk clerk.

She showed him into a small office at the back of reception where he had made the call to the dive boat company the day before. He now phoned the ferry company at Oyster Pond to check that Dick and Penny Irving had been on the passenger list the previous Tuesday, and was told the catamaran had returned on time and the couple had been on it.

"Monsieur Graves," the clerk addressed him as he exited the office. "Lieutenant Latour from the Gendarmerie in Grand Case is on the phone for you." She passed him the receiver.

"Bonjour. Ici Rex Graves."

"*Pierre Latour. Nous venons de recevoir des nouvelles.*"

"News? Regarding Sabine Durand?" Rex asked hopefully.

"*Exactement.* Ze rest of her pareo was picked up early zis morning by a fishing boat, near Ilet Pinel."

"Where is that?"

"It is an island about ten miles north of you. Zey heard on ze news last week how ze actress disappeared from ze beach leaving a piece of her white pareo behind and zey called ze Gendarmerie. Monsieur Bijou, he offered a reward for information. So, you can imagine, we get a lot of crazy calls, but zis one, it is as zey say."

Bless Monsieur Bijou, Rex thought. "Is it a match?"

"Match? *Allumette?*"

"No, not a matchstick. One moment, please." Rex turned to the clerk. "What is the word for when something matches something else?"

"*La même, pareille.*"

"Thank you." Speaking into the phone again, he asked Latour, "Is the fragment from the pareo *pareille* to the one that was found?"

"It appears so. We sent it to ze *laboratoire*. Ze pareo has a part missing which is almost *identique* in shape to ze torn item found on ze beach. It also has a label saying it was fabricated in Tahiti. One of ze guests at ze resort mentioned zis fact."

"It was in Pamela Farley's statement. She remembered that detail because she asked Ms. Durand where she had acquired the pareo. Anything else?"

"No other remains were found around Ilet Pinel. But with ze sharks, zis is to be expected."

"The police searched the area?"

"*Ah, oui, monsieur.* We sent out our Sea Rescue Services at dawn. *Mais rien*—nothing."

"I appreciate you taking the time to inform me of this latest development," Rex told Latour. "*Bonne journée.*"

Why were the gendarmes sticking to the shark theory? It could hardly do the tourist industry much good. But perhaps a shark attack *was* more acceptable than a murder. At least sharks were confined to the sea.

He decided to waste no time in going to see the influential Monsieur Bijou. Of all the people he could think of, the developer had the most clout to reopen the investigation. Rex was all the more intrigued to meet him after what Sean O'Sullivan had said the night before, even though he doubted any of it was true.

Fabulously wealthy men invariably had stories made up about them.

Rex was finally able to track him down at his latest creation, the Marina del Mar, and arrange a meeting that same afternoon. The desk clerk provided him with a map and pointed to Anse Marcel where the exclusive marina was located. The bay, which was just around the coast from Ilet Pinel, looked like a bite taken out of the northernmost part of the island. It wasn't far away and he would ask Paul to lend him the Jeep.

Before setting out, he left a message for Thaddeus in London asking him to research Monsieur Bijou, alias Coenraad van Bijhooven's background, suggesting he look into possible past activities in Amsterdam. Thaddeus, whose services Rex had utilized in his last case, had roomed at Oxford with an undergraduate who now worked for Interpol. If there was any dirt to dig up, Thad would find it. In the meantime, he would meet with Bijou in person and see what could have inspired the Irishman to spin such an improbable tale.

"In case I can't borrow a car, is the hotel limo available for two o'clock?" Rex asked the desk clerk, feeling this might be appropriate transport for his appointment.

"It is booked for the afternoon to take the von Muellers to Philipsburg. I can see if the van is free."

"That's okay." Rex thanked the clerk and made his way to the Winslows' cabana.

Paul unabashedly opened the door in the altogether, holding a mug of coffee.

"Sorry to bother you again, but the limo's taken and I have a meeting with Monsieur Bijou."

"No problem, dear man. Shan't be needing the Jeep today."

"In that case I'll take it now, if I may, and do some sightseeing."

Paul reached back to a table in the hall and pressed the car keys into Rex's hand. "Send dear Mr. Bijou our regards."

Half an hour later, Rex was well on his way. What he appreciated most about St. Martin so far, he reflected as he drove up the coast, was that the island had not broken out in a rash of concrete like so many vacation hotspots around the world—Florida and the Costa del Sol in Spain, to name but a few. He hoped that wouldn't change, but with developers like Bijou putting up luxury high-rises along the coast, who knew?

When he arrived at the Marina del Mar, he found a gated community of six towers soaring from lusciously landscaped islands linked by navigable waterways with individual boat slips and Venetian-style bridges. Rex parked the Jeep in the underground garage of the first tower, as Bijou's personal assistant had instructed on the phone, and entered a lobby tiled in Italian marble. Classical music floated from yucca plants festooning the far corners, while a tubular aquarium in the center disappeared into the cathedral ceiling, soothing the visitor in mind and spirit with its gentle burble and lazy shoals of angelfish.

Impossible to enter the calm and tasteful elegance of the Marina del Mar tower without feeling a sense of entitlement, Rex remarked to himself. He walked over to the V-shaped reception desk where a young woman with Spock eyebrows and subtly applied mauve eye shadow supervised a chrome laptop of ultramodern design. "Rex Graves to see Monsieur Bijou," he informed her.

"I'll let him know you are here," she said in a neutral accent, and spoke into an intercom. "He will see you now, Mr. Graves. Please go up to the penthouse suite."

After summoning one of the transparent elevators, Rex pressed the button for the nineteenth floor. The car rose noiselessly and deposited him at a plush-carpeted antechamber leading to a solid-looking door with a brass knocker. Before he had time to reach for it, a young Adonis of indeterminate race in a white dress suit and black bowtie admitted him into the suite.

"This way, sir," he murmured deferentially, leading Rex onto a wide balcony with panoramic vistas of the private marina and open sea.

A stylish man in his fifties approached, clean-shaven, and with not a silver hair out of place. His eyes were so pale as to be color-less. Even Rex, who had little sartorial *savoir-faire*, could tell that the custom-made suit came from the most expensive cloth, the fabric of the shirt was of the finest linen, and the tie of the rarest silk—platinum gold in color. Rex felt unhappily frumpy in the man's presence. As they shook hands, he was aware of an expensively subtle aftershave emanating from his person.

"Would you care to join me in a gin and tonic?" Monsieur Bijou asked in exquisite English that was yet not quite English.

"Thank you."

"Oscar, please bring the drinks upstairs."

Upstairs? Rex looked about him, certain there could not be another story to the building. Monsieur Bijou gestured to a flight of steps off the balcony, which brought them to a rooftop pool, and indicated a padded patio chair beneath a square umbrella.

"The Marina del Mar is truly an achievement," Rex said, deeming a compliment was in order.

"It was a long time in the making, but, yes, I am pleased with the result," Monsieur Bijou concurred. "We pre-sold 90 percent of the condominiums before we even broke ground. It is a relatively simple matter to buy real estate on the island. There are no special licenses or permits required. You could buy one yourself."

In keeping with his name, Monsieur Bijou wore an ostentatious array of jewels on his manicured fingers: an opal, a sapphire, an emerald—but none on his ring finger. This was probably just as well, since Rex could not begin to imagine what a Madame Bijou would look like. The valet dispensed tumblers garnished with twists of lime.

"Perhaps I'll consider a little *pied-à-terre* on St. Martin when I retire."

"Why wait?" his host asked. "Property values will go up and the sooner you buy, the more time you will have to enjoy it."

"It seems you do very well at practicing what you preach," Rex said, glancing in appreciation about him.

"Indeed, there are so many opportunities. My newest project is a night club in Marigot, which will have a floor show styled after *Les Folies-Bergères*."

"With the Can-Can?"

"But of course. You approve?"

"I'm more familiar with the Highland Fling myself."

Monsieur Bijou smiled urbanely. "There is no comparison. Imagine beautiful semi-naked girls in bright costumes dancing above the footlights, kicking up their legs to the sound of a live Parisian band." He waved a glittering hand as if to conjure up the vision.

"I can see it now." The Tangaray gin helped, adding a nice dry kick to the Schweppes.

"And so to business. Mr. Winslow said he was flying you from Edinburgh to look into the matter of the missing actress. How can I help?"

"It seems you have been of tremendous assistance already."

"A favour for a friend. The least I could do."

A self-interested favor, Rex surmised. Paul Winslow had rich friends who sometimes ended up deciding to purchase property on St. Martin, and he steered them Bijou's way.

"Did you hear that the rest of Ms. Durand's pareo was recovered at sea?" Rex asked.

"I did."

"We must pursue the investigation—"

Monsieur Bijou deposited his glass on the wrought-iron table with a resolute thud. "What does it prove?"

"Only that she ended up in the water. My concern is how she got there."

"Without more evidence, where do we go? The most obvious possibility is that Mademoiselle Durand slipped on the rocks and cut herself, and then foolishly went bathing in the sea at dusk when sharks come inshore to feed." Bijou displayed his rings in another flourish of the hand. "My dear sir, please be at liberty to continue your inquiries, but further insistence on my part with the police would prove fruitless."

"The Gendarmerie report states that she 'in all probability' drowned—if she was not first attacked by sharks."

"There have been other drownings in the area, notably at Galion Beach. Visitors go in the water to cool off and, in some cases, nonswimmers have been overwhelmed by the tide or else have drifted out with the current."

"Ms. Durand was a good swimmer and a certified scuba diver."

"But what proof do you have that it was other than the police suggest?"

"I would like to ascertain the exact cause of death. It would be of comfort to her nearest and dearest."

"Without a body, we may never know for sure." Monsieur Bijou drummed the armrest of his chair with his resplendent fingers. Clearly, he wanted the case dropped. He had been seen to do the right thing by his wealthy friends, and now he wished for the investigation to go away.

"Bodies dead by suspicious means are bad for business?" Rex hazarded.

"Truly, Monsieur Graves, why should this be a suspicious death?" He glanced pointedly at his Rolex.

"Just one more thing. Did you know Sabine Durand?"

"I met her once at a *soirée* in Marigot. She made an indelible impression. Such beauty, such poise—and wit!"

"When was this?"

"Last year, I believe."

Rex knocked back the rest of his gin and tonic. "I know your time is precious. Let me not take up any more of it."

His host showed him into the condo where Oscar escorted him to the front door.

"How long have you worked for Monsieur Bijou?" Rex asked before he walked through it.

Oscar's quick, dark eyes opened wide in a challenge. No point in trying to bribe him for information, Rex realized. The young man had obviously been hired for his strength and his silence. Nothing Rex could pay him would likely compensate the valet for what he stood to gain—or lose—in Bijou's employment.

"Well, good day to you," he said.

"And you, sir."

Rex made his way down the elevator and through the sepulchral splendor of the lobby, feeling only one hundred percent himself once he was back in the Jeep. So much monetary display made him feel nervous.

"What did you think of the Marina del Mar?" Paul inquired when Rex dropped off the car keys half an hour later.

"Impressive."

"I'll say. A bit out of my price league, unfortunately, what with all the renovations we're having done at Swanmere Manor. And how did you find our Monsieur Bijou?"

"Glittery. And as transparent as the diamonds on his cufflinks. I got nothing out of him of any value, though. What's your take on him?"

"Hard to say. I've only ever met him in a formally social context. He's always been very courteous."

"He was less than courteous with me. Almost had his flunky throw me off the premises."

"I suppose he's trying to protect his business interests."

Maybe that was not all he was trying to protect. Rex had the sneaking suspicion the police were in Bijou's pocket and that he was only paying lip service to the rich guests at the resort. Having now met the developer, Rex found himself hoping that Sean O'Sullivan's gossip had substance. He would truly love to knock Midas off his ivory tower.

EIGHT

REX WANDERED BACK TO the office to see if any calls had come in during his trip to Anse Marcel, and was disappointed to find that no news had yet arrived from home. Nor could he wait to receive the information from London, which he had asked to be faxed to the resort at the first opportunity. He decided to call Campbell while he was there.

"How's it going?" his son asked in American fashion.

Rex winced. One year in the States, and his son was already losing his Scottish diction. "Good," he responded in like manner, eschewing the adverb grammatically required by the question.

"Have you caught the bad guy yet?"

"This is only my third day."

"Didn't you solve that case at Swanmere in three days? You must be slipping, Dad."

"Thanks for the vote of confidence. This investigation is trickier as there's no body and very few clues to go on. Actually, I wanted to ask you, since you're studying marine science: Are shark attacks common in the Caribbean?"

"Not as common as in North America or South Africa, where a combination of cold and warm waters brings a large variety of sharks. The Bahamas has recorded more attacks than any other Caribbean destination, but still less than Florida."

"I hope you're being careful." Rex didn't like to think of his son surfing in Florida, yet that had been part of the attraction for Campbell in attending university there.

"It's no more dangerous than mountaineering in the Cairngorms or some other risk-taking adventures I could mention."

"You have a logical argument for everything. You really should've gone into law."

"Dad, don't start on that again."

"Okay, what else can you tell me about sharks?"

"The more surf, the greater the risk of a shark mistaking a human for a fish, especially if the swimmer is wearing shiny jewelry. No, I don't wear jewelry, before you ask."

"I should hope not! Now, Jacques Cousteau, what can you tell me about tides?"

"Look, Dad, I've got a date in a few minutes."

"Just remember who's paying for your education. Please tell me I'm not wasting my money."

He heard his son give a put-upon sigh before launching into his explanation.

"There are usually two high tides and two low tides every day, right? With a little over six hours between high and low tide. Okay so far? The entire tidal cycle repeats itself approximately fifty minutes later each day."

Campbell relayed this information in a bored and superior tone. Rex privately forgave him because the boy was still a teenager and therefore programmed to be obnoxious.

"When the tide has reached it highest and lowest points," his son continued, "there's a brief period when there is no current ebbing or flooding, referred to as slack water. Dad, if you ever went out on boats, you'd know all this."

"I'm no sailor—I get seasick. Glad you're learning something, lad."

"Any chance you can send me some money?"

"I gave you some in Miami."

"I know, but Consuela is high and constant maintenance."

"Find a lass who's lower maintenance."

"You saw her, Dad. She's hot."

"Get a job then."

"Yeah, thanks.

Campbell was losing his Scots accent and all respect. He would never talk to his grandmother like this and risk getting walloped with her bible. Just a year ago, he had been addressing his father as "sir," a habit ingrained by his privileged education at Fettes College in Edinburgh. Ah, well, times were changing, and perhaps just as well, Rex conceded, determined not to be a stick-in-the-mud.

"Take care, son," he said at the end of the call.

Standing at the desk in the small office, he whipped out his pad and pencil and made a brief calculation. The shore had been submerged at seven o'clock the previous evening when he reached the promontory. Working backwards by approximately six and a half hours—eight days times fifty minutes—he calculated that the tide would have been out when Sabine disappeared.

He flipped back through his notes on the guests, beside whose names he had made annotations—further questions he needed to ask, or more information to be gathered on them from other sources. The data on Vernon Powell was spare, to say the least. He was the one guest Rex had not spoken to one-on-one. The general consensus among the guests he'd questioned was that Vernon was jealous and controlling, and prone to fits of violence. Moreover, Rex had promised Winslow that he would try to pry him out of his shell.

Making this his next priority, he walked up to the second cabana but got no answer to his knock at the front door. He banged louder.

"Vernon, it's Rex! I've brought your mail."

Eventually, he heard the sound of bare feet approaching on the tile hallway, and the door opened a foot wide. Vernon stuck his head out. He was shaved and clear-eyed, but gave off the unmistakable scent of rum. Strains of "If I Were a Rich Man" from *Fiddler on the Roof* tumbled through the doorway.

Musicals and opera were not Rex's cup of tea. He found both to be overly dramatic, not to mention unrealistic, in that people were not in the habit of bursting into spontaneous song in everyday life. If he did that in court, he would be summarily disbarred and committed to a mental institution.

"Thanks," Vernon said, taking the day's mail.

"I thought we could have dinner tonight."

Sabine's husband paused for a second, and Rex thought he would find an excuse to refuse. "As long as it's not at The Cockatoo," he said drily.

"Can you recommend anywhere?"

"The California in Grand Case. Good food, great view, and big enough to where we're not likely to run into any of this crowd."

"Right you are. I'll arrange for the hotel to limo us over at seven, if that suits you."

That gave Rex enough time to swim, shower, and read the paper, though the news from home was a day old by the time it reached St. Martin. Returning to his cabana, he changed into his Bermudas and applied a liberal amount of sunscreen. The beach attendants were collapsing the giant yellow umbrellas for the day by the time he arrived. He met the Irvings jogging back from the village side of the beach. Neither had so much as broken into a sweat. They slowed down to a stop.

"Hey, Rex. Haven't seen you all day." Dick, only slightly out of breath, had not a stitch on except for the red and white bandanna. A Yin-Yang symbol, which put Rex in mind of two embracing tadpoles, was tattooed on his smooth chest.

"I've been busy. I went to Anse Marcel to meet with Monsieur Bijou."

"Does he flaunt as many jewels as they say?" Penny asked, cool as a cucumber but for a slight sheen on her nose and between her taut, tanned breasts.

"Aye, every gemstone you can imagine."

"He's quite a legend. I'd love to meet him. Apparently, he's very well groomed."

"Immaculate."

"I heard he had his own masseur."

"Is he gay?" Rex asked.

Dick grinned. "I don't think so. He's popular with the ladies."

"Sabine told me he was bi," Penny contradicted.

"Is that common knowledge?" Rex wanted to know.

"Probably not, but Sabine knew him quite well."

"Really?" Bijou had distinctly said he'd only met her the one time.

"Well, perhaps not *that* well," Penny specified.

"I thought he was a cold fish," Rex concluded, remembering the unusually pale eyes. "Incidentally, I wanted to ask you both what time you got back from your trip to St. Barts last Tuesday."

Dick questioned his wife with a glance. "I wrote down the time in my statement. Let's see, must've been around six-thirty. Can't really remember."

"It was closer to seven," Penny corrected him. "We had to wait for a cab."

"You don't have your own transport?"

"No, we mainly hang out here and take advantage of the beach. St. Barts turned out to be a waste of time, really."

"Did you take a cab to Oyster Pond that morning?"

"Pascal from the hotel took us, but he had the rest of the day off, and the manager was attending Paul's birthday dinner. In any case, what we have to tip him is almost as much as a cab fare."

"You didn't get back in time for the party?"

"We might have managed it but we were pooped," Dick explained. "In any case, we'd already told the others not to expect us before coffee, knowing it would be tight since we had to change first. At around ten, Dave and Toni knocked at our door to see if Sabine was with us."

"We hadn't seen her all day," Penny added. "We went out and looked for her."

"Were you worried?" Rex asked.

Penny pulled the band from her ponytail and redid it. "Not really. I thought she'd forgotten about Paul's dinner and had just gone off somewhere. I remember being annoyed. She was the sort of person who always had to be center stage and create drama around her."

"Yeah, I felt bad for Paul," Dick elaborated. "None of the guests were exactly sober, so the search effort probably wasn't very efficient. Penny and me kinda took over and got the guards from the resort to check out the rocks."

"I'll need to speak with them."

"They're nice local boys," Penny said. "Quite harmless. They mainly just keep out the riff-raff."

As she spoke, a guard in a khaki uniform paced along the sand, a club secured in his belt

"You get the odd voyeur and dope peddler on the beach," Dick explained. "Security only patrols the beach once the umbrella attendants have left. During the day, one guard stays up by the cabanas, out of sight."

"Aye, well, thanks for the information."

"Catch you later," Dick said.

Rex waded into the shallows. Few people remained on the beach, and still less in the sea. Most would be preparing for dinner. Standing waist deep in the water, he gazed at the tiny fish swirling about the sandy bottom. Then, launching himself headlong, he free-styled to the raft anchored in the bay and hoisted himself up the ladder.

The waning sun bathed his face as, from the platform, he surveyed the eight cabanas peeping through the coconut palms and clumps of sea grape, which divided them from the beach. Someone at the resort must know more about Sabine Durand than they were willing to tell.

It was just a matter of probing, applying pressure until the case cracked open along the airtight seam, exposing the dusky secret contained within.

NINE

THE WATERFRONT RESTAURANT RESEMBLED a warehouse in size and structure, which lent a nice airy feel. The entrance displayed shelves of island souvenirs and offered a grouping of sofas where couples sat with drinks from the bar.

"My usual table," Vernon requested of the maître d', who led them to one of the large twilit windows open to the sound of waves lapping on the beach. The lights of Anguilla twinkled in the distance.

"Aye, very nice," Rex said, complimenting Vernon on his choice of restaurant. He scanned the menu and decided on the hot artichoke in gratinated goat cheese sauce and the *coquilles St. Jacques* on curried pasta. In accompaniment, he ordered a bottle of Sancerre. "As you were saying in the limo...," he prompted Vernon, when the waiter left.

"Greg Hastings was at Paul's birthday party at The Cockatoo all evening. He personally organized the whole thing. Then he sat down with us for dinner."

"Unlikely he could have slipped away then."

"There's no way," Vernon said emphatically. "Anyway, I don't suspect him for a minute. For one thing, he isn't Sabine's type. He's managed the resort ever since most of us have been going to the Plage I kept coming after my first wife died. It was less lonely than going on a singles' cruise or to Club Med."

"And the driver?"

"Pascal has worked there for quite a few years as well."

While driving them over to Grand Case, Pascal had told Rex that before his chauffeuring job at the resort, he had worked for a charter boat company, sailing all types of luxury boats for weeks on end. Now he got to sleep most nights at home. He had confirmed he'd had the afternoon and evening off the Tuesday Sabine Durand disappeared. He lived in town with his wife and four children, and had been fishing on his boat until past sunset with his two eldest.

"You should be looking at Brook," Vernon said, wielding his crab cracker, which he then clamped on the crustacean's claw. With one snap, the delicate pink meat was laid bare. "There's an edge to Brook that's not immediately obvious. He has incredible drive. Fact is, he couldn't have made it to where he is without being a son-of-a-bitch when he needed to be."

I'm sure the same could be said of you, Rex thought.

"He was crazy about Sabine." Vernon wiped his fingers off on his napkin. "Well, everybody was. Do you think you'll ever get to the bottom of this case?"

"I certainly intend to try," Rex said, piqued by Vernon's tone. "I'm still at the fact-finding stage. It might help if I could take a look at your wife's personal belongings. Not that I want to impose on your grief…"

"Feel free. I've left everything the way it was. I suppose at the back of my mind I keep thinking she'll come back."

"I don't suppose she took anything with her on her walk?"

"Just what she was wearing, I imagine. How are your scallops?"

Rex was not so easily thrown off the scent. "How was the marriage?" he queried his dinner companion. "Sorry to have to ask."

"I'm just not accustomed to being at the receiving end of the questions." Vernon took a deep breath. "Look, I want to find out what happened to my wife, however painful it might be, but with regard to your question, I didn't feel married to Sabine. She did more or less what she pleased."

"Extramarital affairs?"

"She said not."

"Did the question of divorce ever come up?"

"Of course. I'm sure it does in most marriages."

"Where did you spend most of your time?"

"At our apartment on Park Avenue. Of course, Sabine traveled a lot for her work."

"That can put a strain on a marriage. I expect, as an entertainment attorney, you put a prenuptial agreement in place?"

Something resembling a smile cracked Vernon's wooden face. "Of course."

"And, under the terms of the agreement, how would Sabine have fared?"

"Badly."

Rex was left with no doubt that being on the wrong side of this lawyer would be an extremely uncomfortable place to be. During the main course, they concentrated on the food.

The young waiter cleared away their dinner plates. "Would you care for dessert?" he asked, and listed the selection.

"Why does it always sound so much better in French?" Rex asked in appreciation. "I'm supposed to be on a diet, but I'll make an exception, just tonight."

The waiter smiled. "Very wise."

"The *Crêpes Suzette flambées au Grand-Marnier.*"

"Profiteroles for me," Vernon said.

The waiter nodded and glided away.

"I don't get to eat like this back home," Rex said. "We're rather fond of our haggis and pulverized turnip."

"What is haggis?"

"Sheep's innards."

"Good God." Vernon pulled a sour face.

"The Scots are a thrifty lot. None of the sheep goes to waste."

The waiter drew up a tripod table with a hibachi and set fire to the pancakes in the brass skillet. A deliciously decadent fragrance of torched orange brandy and caramelized sugar wafted into the air. Rex wished he could bottle it and spray it onto his pillow.

Vernon sliced into his chocolate-topped pastry puff filled with French custard. "You can spend a month at the resort and eat out at a different gourmet restaurant every day without ever going into Marigot or Philipsburg."

"Add to that the fantastic weather and the Caribbean Sea. It's paradise all right." Or was, until Sabine Durand went missing, which did lend a sinister pall to the attractions. "Did Sabine take medication of any kind?"

"Only Luminal to help combat jetlag and stagefright."

"What was she seeing the chiropractor about?"

"She got thrown by a horse when she was fourteen and was laid up for a while. Her back plays up from time to time. She says the quack in Philipsburg works wonders."

"Did you ever go there with her?"

"Never. It would've meant a wait at the office and then a shopping expedition afterward. She was always gone at least three hours."

"Did she suffer from depression?"

"You're on the wrong track. She didn't kill herself, if that's what you're getting at."

Rex did not press the point, even though he knew that people closest to the suicide victim often went into denial over the subject. Still, by all accounts, Sabine did not appear to be a likely candidate for suicide, unless there was some mental illness she kept quiet about. The police had made only a perfunctory search of the cabana.

"How did you come to lose your phone on the beach that night?"

"I didn't. It was in our cabana. I remember checking my messages before I went on the dive excursion. Later, when I wanted to see if Sabine had called, I couldn't find it."

"This was before the party?"

"Yes, while I was waiting for my wife to make an appearance. In the end, I left without her."

The waiter poured them the rest of the wine from the ice bucket. Vernon thawed slightly when they moved away from the topic of Sabine to discuss the differences between American and Scottish law, intrigued to learn that courts in Scotland have fifteen jurors, as opposed to twelve in the States.

"Another important aspect of Scots law," Rex told him, "is that every essential fact has to be corroborated by two independent witnesses."

"Interesting," Vernon said. "Harder to prove guilt."

"Aye, but our law allows three verdicts: guilty, not-guilty, and not-proven. Not-proven means that though the prosecution failed to meet the criterion of 'beyond reasonable doubt,' there is still a suspicion of guilt in the jury's mind and in the mind of the public."

"That's how I feel—as though my friends were the jury and, in default of being proven guilty beyond reasonable doubt, I'm walking around in a cloud of suspicion."

"We'll see if we can't clear that up," Rex told him. *You canny old lawyer.*

The limo picked them up at nine prompt.

"I'll be playing racquet ball with Duke in the morning," Vernon informed Rex on the drive back to the resort. "You can come to my cabana then and poke around Sabine's things to your heart's content."

"Thanks. It'll give me a better feel for her."

"I wish you could have met her."

"I do too. She sounds intriguing."

They bid each other a cordial goodnight outside the cabanas. When Rex opened his door, Brooklyn met him in the hallway and handed him a message from the front desk.

"I just got back and found this on the door," his roommate said. "I was about to go looking for you."

"I went to dinner in Grand Case." Thinking the message might be from Thaddeus in London, Rex was eager to read it. "URGENT," it said. "Call mother."

"Do you want to use my cell phone?" Brooklyn asked.

Rex glanced at his watch, rubbing it absentmindedly with his thumb. "It's past two in the morning in Scotland."

"But if it's urgent…"

"Aye. Thanks, I will borrow your phone if you dinna mind. I'm not getting service on mine out here."

"You'll have to take it outside to get a signal," Brooklyn said, handing him the Motorola. "Just don't let anyone see you. They're a bit uptight around here about finding their nude pictures on some sleazy website."

Rex privately considered most of them had nothing to worry about, unless they were concerned about being blackmailed.

"Could be embarrassing, I guess," Brooklyn said, voicing his thoughts. "Hope everything's okay," he added, discretely disappearing into his room.

The message had been taken almost three hours ago, far past his mother's bedtime. Anxiously, he dialed her number.

"This is the Graves residence," the housekeeper in Edinburgh intoned on the recording. "Please leave a message for Moira Ann Graves or Rex Graves, QC."

Rex started speaking in the hope his mother would pick up. If the news was that urgent, she would have waited up for his call—although she was getting on now and was prone to nodding off. "I'll try you first thing in the morning my time, Mother," he ended by saying into the machine.

He wandered back in from the patio and knocked at Brooklyn's door.

"Couldn't get through?" the American asked, tying the belt of his white bathrobe.

"I got the answering machine."

"Keep the phone with you so you can try again later. Leave it on the kitchen counter when you're done with it."

"I appreciate it. My mother will be up in three or four hours. She's an early riser."

"Is she in good health?" Brooklyn asked.

"Aye, fit as a fiddle, but she's eighty-five. The message might be regarding my friend in Iraq. I haven't heard from her in a while."

"Is she Iraqi?"

"No, she went to Baghdad on a humanitarian mission. She disappeared from her hotel without leaving a forwarding address and I can't get through to the relief office where she works."

"That's tough," Brooklyn said sympathetically. "Here, let me make you a pot of coffee. Looks like it's going to be a long night."

Rex followed him into the living room. "You don't need to go to the trouble."

"No trouble." Brooklyn filled the machine with water and within minutes the kitchen was filled with an appetizing aroma of freshly ground French roast.

"It's just that with all the bombings over there, I don't know what's going on from one day to the next."

Brooklyn leaned against the counter. "Have you contacted your Embassy?"

"Aye. She's not on any casualty list. I suppose what concerns me most is the risk of kidnapping. Several hundred people of all nationalities, religions, and professions have been kidnapped since April of last year. Even the Red Cross and the UN are targets. And Moira goes into areas where there's not always a military presence."

"Moira? Is that a Scottish name?"

"Aye. It's my mother's name as well, which gets confusing."

Brooklyn pulled two mugs from an upper cabinet. "I heard you had a son in Florida…"

"Campbell. He just finished his first year at Hilliard University in Jacksonville. Marine Science."

"Cool. Milk, sugar?"

"Both, ta very much." Rex sighed out of disillusionment. "I did rather hope he'd go into law."

"Follow in his father's footsteps, huh?" Brooklyn set a mug of steaming coffee on the counter beside Rex and poured one for himself. "My one regret is not having kids," he said. "Once I meet the right woman, I will though."

"Did no one ever fit that description?" Rex did not wish to seem indelicate in light of what Brooklyn had told him about his feelings for Sabine, but the companionship fostered by the urgent message from his mother, the time of night, and the two of them sharing a place in the French West Indies made him forego his usual reserve and sense of propriety.

"Oh, if you're referring to Sabine," Brooklyn said candidly, "there was never any question of kids. She always said she wasn't built for it. Well, you saw in the picture how skinny she was."

"Many a brawny bairn was born of a slender lass," Rex countered. "When Fiona, my late wife, was carrying Campbell, the doctor warned she might have to have a caesarian due to her narrow hips. But she was delivered of a healthy nine-pound boy after less than three hours in labour, without the necessity of surgical intervention."

She had failed to win the battle against breast cancer, however. Rex gulped his coffee to force down the bitter lump rising in his throat.

"I think it was probably vanity on Sabine's part," Brooklyn concluded. "In any case, kids would have gotten in the way of her career."

"What's the name of that American actress who adopted children from third-world countries?"

"Angelina Jolie?"

"Aye. Very admirable. Moira has often talked about adopting a child. She said not to be surprised if she brought one back from Iraq."

"How would you feel about that?"

"That would be just grand." Rex swirled the dregs at the bottom of his mug. What he said was true enough, but he wondered if raising an orphan would in fact ultimately fulfill Moira's indefatigable capacity for self-sacrifice. There had been times when he felt unable to keep up.

"Vernon would have liked kids, I think," Brooklyn said, pouring the remains of his coffee down the sink. "Have you had a chance to interview him yet?"

"We spoke over dinner. He's an astute man."

"Yeah, not so easy to manipulate."

"What d'you mean by that?"

"Sabine couldn't exactly twist him around her little finger the way she could with other men."

Yawning uncontrollably, Rex took another look at his watch. "I'll try to grab a couple of hours' sleep and then call my mother again. Thanks for the loan of your phone."

"Hey, don't sweat it. Wake me if you need to talk."

Rex thanked him and went to prepare for bed. It was a horrible feeling to crave sleep and know you would be unable to succumb to its blissful release. He switched on the ceiling fan, lay down on his bed half-dressed, and turned off the light, letting his mind dance to any tune his thoughts struck up, mostly morbid ones where a blindfolded Moira was being forced at gunpoint to plead for her life and denounce her country's support for the war. Or on another ominous note, his mother had just been diagnosed with a terminal illness—or perhaps Miss Bird, their devoted housekeeper, had taken a fall down the stairs.

Rex rolled over on his side. He could just make out the outline of Helen's postcard on the nightstand. A soothing melody calmed his nerves as he recalled her words.

"… *went ahead and booked my passage on the Sun-Fun Cruise Line. Will dock at St. Martin on July 23rd. Meet me off the* Olympia…"

He fell asleep at that point, but tossed fretfully for the next couple of hours, the import of the late-night call from his mother running like a dark thread through his troubled dreams.

TEN

AT FIVE-THIRTY REX AWOKE with a start. Jumping off the bed, he stumbled onto the back patio and dialed his mother's number in Edinburgh. It was so quiet outside he could hear the lapping of waves on the powdered sand beyond the grayed-down colors of the predawn.

"Mother!" he almost shouted when her voice answered. "I got your message to call. I tried late last night."

"How are ye, Son? You sound croaky. Are ye coming down wi' something?"

"I just got up. I've been worried sick—"

"Nay, lad, it isna bad, I dinna think."

"What isn't?" Rex asked, experiencing a meteoric rise in his blood pressure.

"It's about Moira—"

"You heard from her!"

"A letter arrived."

"What does it say?"

"Well, I didna open it! It's addressed to you."

"Oh, fer goodness' sake, open it, will ye?" Rex said, emotion thickening his Scots accent. His hand on the cell phone started shaking. He gripped it more tightly.

"Are ye sure?"

"Mother," he said in a stern voice. He heard the tearing of paper at the other end of the connection and then a lengthy pause. "Is it a long letter?" he asked.

"Noo, it's just that…"

"What?" His mother's reticence alarmed him. Perhaps Moira had uncharacteristically added some intimate language to her missive, and his mother was standing by the phone in the hall, stricken with shock. Sex was never a topic of conversation in the house.

"She's run off!" his mother finally said in disbelief.

"Run off where?" Moira was already in Iraq. How much farther could she run?

"Run off wi' another man!"

"Who?"

"His name's Dillon. He works for a paper in Sydney."

"Mother, read me the letter."

"Well, I shall, but it's shameful. She writes, 'Dearest Rex, please forgive me for not writing before. I tried so many times, but it was not easy to say what I had to, and the pressure of work here is enormous, as you know. More on that later. I've met someone. We didn't mean for it to happen, but it's God's will. He pulled me out from under a pile of rubble. Through the smoke I saw a pair of blue eyes peering at me with concern and—'"

"That's enough. I get the picture."

"Aye, it reads like a Barbara Taylor Bradford novel. There's no even a return address. So, anyway, what's it like out there in the French West Indies?" his mother asked, attempting to distract him from the bad news.

Rex got a hold of himself. "There are bays and inlets with white sand beaches and palm trees," he replied without enthusiasm, averting his eyes from the blaze of yellow just now breaking through the amber sky. "It's straight out of *Treasure Island*. The food is mostly spicy or French, sometimes a mixture of both."

"It sounds so exotic. What about the people?" His mother always wanted to know about people.

"The islanders have gentle features and happy dispositions."

"I canna be surprised they'd be happy the way you describe the place. What is there to do?"

"Just about any water sport, horseback riding, shopping." Rex thought it best not to mention the naturist attractions and risk getting a sermon.

"I am sorry about Moira."

"Aye, but I knew it couldna be good news after so long. It's still better than finding out she got kidnapped or blown up." *Just barely*.

"What about that nice woman who called from Derby? The one you met at Christmas at Swanmere Manor? She sounded so pleasant on the phone."

"Helen d'Arcy. She sent me a postcard saying she'd be stopping on St. Martin next week for the day. She's on a Caribbean cruise."

"Well, I'm glad aboot that. I have to say I'm verra disappointed in Moira Wilcox. Running off wi' a photographer! The ones on TV look so scruffy. And she's so straight-laced. I just canna credit it."

"It's different out there, Mother. There's a war going on."

"I suppose you're right. And I'm glad you're taking it well. When are ye going to bring Helen to tea?"

"I'll have to see how things go when I see her."

"It may all turn out for the best," his mother said cheerfully. "Have you been in touch wi' Campbell?"

"We spoke yesterday. He sends his love."

"I wish the lad would write more."

"He probably would if he could e-mail you."

"E-mail! At my age."

His mother could not even fathom the television remote, and so Rex refrained from extolling the convenience of computer technology. Imagining her in front of a laptop was as incongruous as picturing a robot taking tea at a table set with his mother's lace doilies.

"Reginald?"

"Mother?"

"Reread the Gospel according to Matthew, chapter eleven, verses 28 through 30. It will make your suffering easier to bear."

"Aye, Mother."

However, in the event, he did not resort to the scriptures. Leaving Brooklyn's phone on the counter, he strode back through the sliding glass doors in a frigid blue fury. The sand felt hard and cool beneath his pounding feet. He barely noticed when he stood on a burr. The beach, deserted and devoid of the vibrant color of later morning, looked unwelcoming, but the water was just beginning to glimmer with promise. He ripped off his briefs, abandoning them on the shore, and splashed into the sea as fast as the resistance of the water permitted.

We didn't mean for it to happen, but it's God's will.

Moira's echoing words infuriated him. How many times had he heard "God made me do it" as an excuse in court? God must be incensed by all the stupid feeble excuses dumped at his feet. Rex swam parallel to the beach, his strong strokes tugging the sea out of the way as he furiously blinked the salt from his eyes. When he reached the promontory, he U-turned under the water and returned the way he had come, using his cabana as a landmark, the vigorous exercise gradually driving all meaningful thought from his brain.

Och, that's better, he thought, flinging his upright legs through the shallows to where his cotton briefs lay unceremoniously tossed on the sand. Realizing he had forgotten his towel, he used them to brush off the excess moisture from his body. He spotted Paul and Elizabeth on their patio at the third cabana and gave a peremptory wave before hurrying back to his place, loosely holding the underwear in front of his privates.

After rinsing off under the outdoor shower, he went inside to shave, and then lingered over a Sudoku puzzle while drinking his coffee. The puzzle took longer than usual since his mind kept wandering back to Moira. He still had trouble believing the news.

Brooklyn wandered onto the patio in his bathrobe, yawning and stretching. He looked even better with dark stubble, Rex noticed with envy. His own chin sprouted ginger hairs and he had bedhead first thing in the morning.

"There's coffee in the pot," he informed Brooklyn.

"Thanks. Did you get your news?"

"Aye, nobody died but me. My girlfriend left me for another man—a photographer from Down Under." Rex reported the facts and even managed to make them sound humorous.

"Good *on* ya, mate," Brooklyn commiserated in an Australian accent. "Plenty more fish in the sea."

When nine o' clock rolled around, Rex went next door and, poking his head into Vernon's hallway, called out "Hello!" to see if the lawyer had left for his game of racquet ball.

Hearing no response, he penetrated the cabana and glanced around the living room, which contained little in the way of personal effects other than a stack of CDs and a pile of American entertainment magazines. He opened the door to one of the two bedrooms, to all appearances uninhabited and with the bed made, but when he looked in the wall-to-wall closet, he found a rack full of clothes. For a moment, he doubted these could belong to Sabine. Though stylish enough, most of the dresses did not entirely live up to what he pictured a glamorous young actress would wear.

He read a label, not recognizing the designer's name—not that he was an expert on women's clothes, but he was familiar with Versace and von Furstenberg, and he even remembered Emanuel, the husband and wife team that had made Princess Diana's wedding dress. Clearly none of these clothes was of that caliber. The size of one dress caught his eye: a six? Surely that was too big for a willowy lass. The bulk of them, he discovered, were twos. Perhaps she had put on weight since the riding photo.

Or perhaps she was expecting to. What if the chiropractor she was seeing was another sort of doctor? Whatever was going on, Vernon seemed unaware of it. Rex decided to leave the questions for now and continue his search.

The built-in safe in the closet was unlocked. Rex rummaged through the jewelry, none of it worth as much as he would have expected. *A frugal lass*, he approved. His son's Cuban girlfriend could take a leaf out of Sabine's book. All the same, he felt something was wrong. The items did not match his impressions of their owner.

Next he searched the bathroom, finding nothing of note, but appreciative of the fragrance of the lemon sherbet bar soap by the sink, provided courtesy of the resort.

The suite across the hall accommodated only Vernon's belongings. Little the wiser, Rex headed toward the front door. As he was leaving, the maid, a statuesque woman in her forties with handsome ebony features, approached, rolling her cleaning cart along the path.

"Okay to go in?" she asked.

Rex held the door open. "Aye, no one's home."

Afraid she might think he'd been snooping, which in effect he had, he was about to explain his presence.

"Is maid service to Monsieur's satisfaction?" she asked.

"Oh, aye. The cabanas are spotless."

Outside, he caught sight of a guard patrolling the far perimeter of the resort. Deciding to keep busy so he wouldn't think of Moira, Rex crossed the grounds.

A six-foot wire fence concealed by a hedge closed off the property from the open land beyond, which ended at the dirt road leading to the Sundown Ranch and Butterfly Farm.

"Mind if I walk with you?" he asked the beefy guard.

"I seen you round. You dat lawyer from Scotland." He introduced himself as Winston and said he would be glad to answer any questions.

"Thank you." Rex fell into step with him as he toured the outdoor tennis and indoor racquet ball courts. "How many guards work here?"

Winston informed him there were three, who rotated. He then volunteered the information that he and a younger man called Pierre had been working the night shift when Sabine Durand disappeared.

"What time did you arrive for work?"

"Just before six. We went to da front office as we always do. Da desk manager gives us a briefing before we go on patrol to tell us what to look out for. Da Gendarmerie sends reports to da resort about any crime in da area."

"Was it quiet that night?"

"Very quiet. I din' know what was up till da Canadian man with tattoos come running up an' say we have to search for da young lady. Den *ev'rybody* was rushing about. Pierre an' me went past da rocks. Was too dark to see anyting, but dere wasn't no body. Next morning I had to stay until da po-lice come."

"Who found Mr. Powell's cell phone?"

"I did, over by da rocks."

"Did you see Pierre on patrol?"

"We walk a circle in different directions. One goes front of da cabanas, other goes down da beach, an we meet up in da middle an continue. Ev'ry five rounds, we stop for a cigarette an' rest for a while."

"Where do you take your cigarette break?"

"Back of da Cockatoo, by da kitchens. After ten, we get a meal. I was goin' over dere when I heard about da missing woman."

When Rex spoke to Pierre, who was on guard at the front entrance, the shy youth repeated everything his colleague had said, though less eloquently. He hadn't understood whom they were looking for until he saw the papers and recognized Mlle. Durand from the resort.

"Any strange goings-on in the last couple of weeks that you remember?" Rex asked.

Pierre shook his head, a blank look on his face. Rex thanked him and went inside the main building, where he was pleased to find a message from Thaddeus waiting for him at the front desk. At last. He asked Danielle if he might use the phone in the back office to call London.

"This could be important," he said.

ELEVEN

"Browne, Quiggley, and Squire," the young law clerk answered. "Mr. Quiggley's office."

"Thad, 'tis I," Rex announced.

"Oh, good, sir. I have quite a bit of information for you."

"Thanks for getting to it so fast. What did you find out?"

"Well, here are the salient facts, Mr. Graves, sir. I'll fax the entire report as soon as we're off the phone."

Rex heard a preparatory cough. Thaddeus was still a bit wet behind the ears and had a lot to learn, but he was a thorough researcher.

"Coenraad van Bijhooven, alias Bijou," the law clerk began, "was born in Amsterdam in 1957. His mother, Alice Frankel, was a high-class call girl who gave up her profession to marry Henrick van Bijhooven, a successful industrialist. Coenraad went to Paris to read international law at the Sorbonne."

"Did he now?" Rex asked pensively.

"Upon his return to Holland, he went into the flesh trade and opened a string of strip clubs in the Amsterdam red light district, which he sold fifteen years ago to set up in real estate on St. Martin. When his father died, he left Coenraad a sum of money which provided capital for some of his more ambitious projects."

"Did you manage to link him to the Jewel Murders in Amsterdam?"

"A couple of witnesses came forward at the time but their silence must have been bought off because they never appeared in court. The girls, who were found sexually assaulted, tortured, and bejeweled, had all worked for Coenraad as either prostitutes or dancers. I did find out an interesting fact."

"Go on."

"They were all of slender build, with long hair and delicately modeled cheekbones."

The description evoked an image of Sabine.

"The women resembled his mother," Thaddeus informed him. "There's a picture in the file."

"Is she still alive?"

"No. A complication arose when she was delivering her second child. Both mother and baby died while Coenraad was in Paris."

"Have there been any murders on the island with the same *modus operandi* as those in Amsterdam?"

"Two years ago. Both investigations fizzled to nothing. It was widely assumed a tourist was responsible and then left the island. The victims were not found immediately. Their relative states of decomposition showed they were murdered within a couple of weeks of each other."

"Who were they?"

"One worked as an exotic dancer at The Stiletto in Philipsburg."

A chill ran down Rex's spine, alerting him to the fact that he might be on to something. "Owned by Bijou?"

"Correct. He changed his name legally before he left Holland, and travels on his new passport."

"What do we know about the girls?"

"Leona Couch was in her twenties. The other victim was a tour guide: Geraldine Linder, early thirties. Both fit descriptions of the women in Amsterdam."

"What was the connection between Bijou and the tour guide?"

"None was ever established. I'll fax the report right now. It's marked for your attention and has CONFIDENTIAL stamped all over it. Stand by."

Rex had often thought Thaddeus should have gone into the Secret Service, but the studious young man was not exactly the field agent type.

"I'll wait by the machine. And thank you verra much. Next time I'm in London, I'll take Quig out to dinner and extol your virtues."

Quiggley was one of the partners at the firm Thaddeus clerked for, and a longtime friend of Rex's.

"I'd appreciate that, sir. And good luck with the case. I hope you'll let me know the outcome."

"Never fear. Good day to you, lad."

For a brief moment, Rex whimsically thought how nice it would be to have a son like Thaddeus, whom he could mentor in law, and who spent more time studying and therefore less time chasing women than Campbell.

He exited the office and addressed the desk clerk. "Would you do me a favour and make an appointment for me to see this chiropractor while I wait for a fax?" Handing her the message slip that had been in Vernon's pigeon-hole, he returned to the fax machine which was just beginning to spurt out the pages of Thad's report.

"The phone number for the chiropractor in Philipsburg does not exist," the clerk told him when he came back out of the office, report in hand.

"Are you sure it was taken down correctly?"

"*Absoluement, monsieur.* I took the number down on several messages."

"Do you have a directory handy?"

She placed the "Yellow Pages Sint Maarten" for the Dutch side of the island on the desk. Rex scanned the listings for Dr. Sganarelle and found no one by that name. He then checked the local phone book to no avail.

"Thanks," he said, closing the book.

Entering the store in the building to buy breakfast, he encountered Greg Hastings, the resort manager, who wore a brass badge to that effect. A nattily dressed man with a neatly trimmed salt-and-pepper beard, he greeted Rex effusively and asked how he was enjoying his stay at La Plage d'Azur.

"Verra pleasant." Rex asked the manager about the two guards.

"The employees are all carefully vetted," he assured Rex in a northern English accent. "We only take on people we can trust and whom other employees can vouch for. Uh-oh," he said glancing out the window. "Rain's coming."

Rex looked out at the sky, which was dark to the east. Raindrops began to fall.

"It doesn't usually last long," Hastings assured him.

"Winston told me he was the one who found the phone belonging to Mr. Powell."

"That's right. He gave it to me and I put it in the safe overnight. The gendarmes confiscated it the next morning but returned it a few days later after Mr. Powell made a huge fuss about it having all his clients' numbers on it and needing it for work." The manager's pale face colored slightly.

"Is there something you want to tell me?"

"I'm afraid you're going to think very badly of me."

"Not if you come clean now," Rex encouraged, hoping for a promising confession.

"Well..." Hastings stuck his hands in his jacket pockets. "While I was waiting for Mr. Powell to pick up his phone, I was idly comparing the functions to mine. All right, I admit it, I was curious about what big-shot entertainment clients he might have. But I would never divulge what I found."

The manager paused, but Rex didn't do him the favor of asking for names, since he personally had little interest in American stars, except perhaps for Angelina Jolie.

"Anyway," Hasting continued. "A photo came up on the phone. Most of them were boring sightseeing pics. None of Mr. Powell's gorgeous wife, it was interesting to note. Just rock formations and such. Vernon likes geology. He's so stony-faced himself, he probably feels there's a connection."

Rex smiled in spite of himself and waited for what the manager had to tell him.

"I downloaded the photo because it looked suspicious. It was the last one taken before the phone was found on the beach, and was dated July 10. Lieutenant Latour never pursued it. I suppose he failed to see the relevance, but I made a photocopy. Wait here a sec."

Hastings returned with a sheet of paper. "See what you make of this."

Rex examined the photocopy, which took up a quarter of the sheet of paper. The photo, taken at night, looked at first glance like a grainy blur of indistinct shapes. "I canna tell what it is," he said.

"Look carefully."

Rex blinked to refresh his eyes and get a different perspective, as when contemplating one of those *trompe l'oeils* that can either represent a vase or two facing profiles, depending on how you view it.

"Ah, now I see," he said. "It's part of a woman's face taken from below. I recognize the necklace."

"It belongs to Mrs. Winslow. I don't think she meant to be in the photo, not from that angle."

The digitalized date stamp confirmed the photo was taken the day Sabine Durand disappeared. What was Elizabeth doing on Vernon's cell phone that same night? "Did Winston say exactly where he found the phone?"

"This side of the promontory, up by the rocks. He noted the location and time in his report: 10:24 p.m. Do you want to keep the photocopy?"

"I don't think so, but put it somewhere safe for now. You've been verra cooperative."

"If Mrs. Winslow found the phone, why did she leave it on the beach?"

"Good question."

Pondering this new development, Rex made his purchases at the boutique-cum-grocery. On his way out of the main building, he saw Duke Farley hurrying over from the direction of the racquet ball court, a white towel draped around his squat neck.

"Good work-out?" Rex asked from the top step, just as the rain started in earnest, drumming on the porch roof.

Duke ran up the steps for cover. "You bet. D'you play?"

The curly blond hair on his thick torso glistened with rain and sweat. Rex considered what it must be like running energetically about the court with everything swinging.

"I have no eye-hand coordination."

"What do you do for exercise?"

"I like to hike. Gives me a chance to nature-watch."

A leering grin spread over the Texan's face. "Nature, huh? Well, you sure came to the right place. What ya think of the local talent?"

Rex wondered if he was referring to the band at The Cockatoo, which he couldn't rate, not having much of an ear for music.

"The babes," Duke prompted. "If you go down by the bars at the other end of the beach, ya'll see some that are barely legal."

Rex failed to understand what a beautiful and intelligent woman like Pam saw in Duke Farley, but apparently he was worth billions in oil and beef. Rex appraised him again with a swift glance. Oil and beef was precisely what he was. He could not help but feel an aversion for the man.

"Yessir, plenty of bathing beauties at La Plage. Now, Sabine, there's a gal that looked good wet."

"Excuse me?"

"The true test of beauty. Some women just look good wet."

"Oh—aye." The vision of Ursula Andress emerging seductively from the sea, blonde hair slicked back as droplets of water beaded her womanly form, had fueled many a moment of lonely adolescent lust since Rex first saw the James Bond movie.

"What a waste," Duke said, shaking his large head. "What'll you do if you find out who the murderer is?"

"Hand him or her over to the authorities."

Duke snorted. "Like they'll do anything."

"My mandate is to unearth the culprit if I can. I canna enforce justice. In any case, this half of the island is part of an overseas department of France and therefore subject to French law."

"Bad luck for Sabine," the Texan growled. "Oh, hell, this rain might last a while. See ya around." Pulling the towel over his head, he ploughed into the deluge.

Bad luck for Sabine, indeed, Rex thought, glumly munching on his croissant while he decided whether to make a run for it too.

How could he get his hands on the elusive Bijou? Where could he get proof of his guilt? Horrible to think the young actress could be another victim in a string of bizarre international killings.

TWELVE

REX CADGED A LIFT into Philipsburg in Brooklyn's jeep, a newer Japanese model than Paul Winslow's, though no more roomy inside.

"Where did you say you wanted to be dropped off?" Brooklyn asked on the way into the Dutch capital.

"The Stiletto Night Club."

"The strip joint?" his roommate asked in surprise. "I don't think it's open at lunchtime. It's not one of those seedy dives either. You have to wear a suit and tie to get in."

Rex was wearing a casual short-sleeved shirt. "I'm not going for my own pleasure." He had only ever been to one strip show, and that had been for a college friend's stag night in Glasgow, a less than glamorous experience best forgotten. "I'm following a lead. Sounds like you might know where I can find the place."

"It's not far from the port."

Rex thought it natural that a young bachelor of the world like Brooklyn would know The Stiletto, and tried not to hold it against him.

They entered the narrow streets of the commercial district and became ensnarled in stop-and-go traffic. Office workers and tourists with shopping bags crossed between the stalled cars. No one appeared to be in a hurry.

"What are the girls like there? I'm only asking because I heard one of them was murdered a few years ago."

"Couldn't really tell you as it's been a while since I was there. That's one of Bijou's clubs and I tend to avoid him."

"Why's that?"

"I was dating a young woman called Gerry from this side of the island," Brooklyn replied. "I even brought her to La Plage once or twice. That was two years ago. Anyway, I discovered she was two-timing me with that effeminate jerk Bijou."

"So you ditched her."

"I can't remember who ditched who, but she went back to Europe. Ships passing in the night. It was no big deal." Brooklyn pulled into a small parking lot by a government building. "I'll have to drop you off here as I'm late for my meeting. The Stiletto is down that street all the way to your left. How will you get back to the resort?"

"I'll call the hotel desk when I'm finished, or else get a cab. See you back there."

He followed the directions Brooklyn had given him and arrived at The Stiletto, a whitewashed building wedged between two office blocks and displaying a black high-heeled shoe across the white double doors, which turned out to be locked.

Rex had not called in advance, not wishing to alert Bijou of his intention to nose around and question some of his minions. Coming later when people would be too busy to talk to him had not made sense either, so now he was pretty much stuck as to how to proceed—until he noticed a small side door for deliveries. He turned the handle and the door opened.

Following a corridor to the back of the building, he ended up in a kitchen equipped with gleaming stainless steel surfaces. A double swing door led into a restaurant decked out in elegant black-on-crimson décor, with spotlights focused on three daises for the dancers. A cherry wood counter extended the width of the back wall.

A bartender sat on a stool poring over a ledger. Rex coughed politely to announce his presence, and the man spun around.

"Are you lost?" he asked sternly, with a faint German or Dutch accent, no doubt assuming Rex had wandered in off the street, and annoyed at being disturbed.

Rex realized he must be the bar manager. "I'm not a tourist. I came to ask a few questions regarding Monsieur Bijou."

"You are from the police?"

"No, I'm a lawyer pursuing an investigation." Rex handed him his business card.

The man looked unimpressed.

"I just need to know one thing: where your boss was two weeks ago Tuesday."

"He was here that night."

"Can you prove it?"

"Actually, yes. I have him on security tape entering the building. You are quite welcome to see it." The man glanced around him and, satisfied that they were alone, said in a low voice. "Look, I don't owe Bijou any favours other than my paycheck. I'm not covering for the guy, if that's what you're thinking. Every other Tuesday he comes in at six o'clock, meets with the accountant, and stays for the show. In fact, he's due here again this Tuesday, so I'm going over the books just to make sure they are in order. If there are any anomalies, he'll find them. He has X-ray vision."

"I know. I met him," Rex said, hoping the tape would not exonerate the slippery bastard.

"How do I know you are not really a reporter?"

"Why would I be?"

"We get them sniffing around all the time. Bijou is newsworthy. He's always doing something for the community or hanging out with the elite."

"Aye, he seems to keep quite busy. He was telling me about his new nightclub in Marigot. Says it'll rival anything in Paris."

"He will make it happen. People will flock to Marigot."

"I suppose The Stiletto was a big attraction when it first opened."

"I wouldn't know. I have been here less than two years. Monsieur Bijou tends not to keep his managers very long."

"Why is that?"

"He doesn't like people knowing too much about his business."

"Is there something shady going on?"

The man stood up and rounded the bar. "Can I get you a soft drink?" he asked, spritzing soda into a glass for himself.

"I'm fine, thanks."

The manager swept an arm around the mirrored walls and chandeliers of the cabaret lounge. "This is just show. His real money is in gemstones. Liquid assets. He has a flawless eye. He wears a million dollars on his fingers alone, including a rare Larimar of pure lagoon blue."

"Hence the bodyguard."

The bar manager scrutinized him across the polished wood counter. "He has many baboons. Oscar. Nito. Sergei. I cannot tell you anything more."

"I understand. I'd just like to see the tape."

The man shrugged. "Come with me."

Rex followed him down the corridor into an office that doubled up as a storeroom. Extracting a cassette tape from a shelf, he ran it for Rex.

"Satisfied?" he asked as Bijou's image on screen disappeared beneath the camera on his way through the entrance.

"Unfortunately, yes."

He had hoped to rule out the resort guests as suspects. Now he was back at square one.

THIRTEEN

THE WEEKS INVITED HIM to a cook-in at their cabana on Saturday night. Since David was a cordon bleu chef, the dinner promised to be special, especially as the ingredients were to be purchased fresh from the Marigot market that morning. The couple persuaded Rex to go with them to the French capital, which he had passed through when he first arrived.

"Marigot's a bit provincial," Toni told him as Pascal ferried them across the countryside in the limo. "But it's colourful."

She wore large dark sunglasses and a white linen dress that set off her exotic looks. Her husband, seated beside her, was vastly improved in street clothes as well. When they arrived, Pascal dropped the three of them off and went to get breakfast at the Café Terrace, where they arranged to meet up later.

The market, a short walk from the town center, blended a relaxed European and Caribbean flair. Tourists and locals bartered with merchants displaying tropical fruit and vegetables beneath bleached canvas canopies. Ripe produce, incense, saffron, and curry powder mingled with the tang of fish and salt air. On the sea front, pelicans dove for scraps from the morning's catch. David wandered off toward the boats to purchase mahi-mahi and shrimp.

Meanwhile, Rex could not find anything that might appeal to his mother. Circulating the souvenir stalls in Toni's company, he pictured Moira and her Australian lover arm-in-arm at a Baghdad market—a risky place to be, considering all the bomb and mortar attacks—but no doubt the danger lent an edge to their whirlwind romance. He was in no doubt that the rugged Aussie was her lover. "*Blue eyes peering through the smoke*" did not portend well for a platonic relationship.

He consoled himself that Moira, a smart and hitherto discerning woman, probably already regretted sending him the Dear John letter. Not that he would take her back now. *No, Moira Wilcox, ye made your bed and on it ye shall lie.* He determined to waste no further thought on her and considered instead how refreshing it would be to see Helen again, a lass with a quick sense of humor and down-to-earth good sense—and blue eyes to match those of any wallaby from Down Under. He was glad now about her last-minute decision to join the group of teachers from her school on a cruise. She had flown to Puerto Rico to board the flagship *Olympia* a few days before he left for St. Martin and was now steaming toward him at full speed.

"What about this bird feeder for your mother?" Toni suggested, holding out a hand-carved coconut on a rope.

"Aye, she likes birds, but we live in a Victorian terraced house with only a narrow wee garden, and I'm not sure a coconut would fit in. She has verra traditional tastes."

"How about some Magic Spice then?"

"What's that?"

"It's what's going on the mahi-mahi tonight. Dave claims it contains pot."

"Our housekeeper would never use anything like that. She might get addicted and she's forgetful enough as it is."

"I meant for your mother."

"Och, she doesna cook. She's too busy with her charities and, to be quite honest, to inflict her cooking on anybody would be an uncharitable act in itself."

"Well, maybe one of these silk shawls with fringes." Toni expertly whipped through the hangers exhibiting a shimmering array of color.

"Aye," Rex exclaimed. "That would be just the ticket."

He knew it would end up adorning a table in one of the guest bedrooms, but his mother would appreciate the gesture nevertheless. Taking Toni's advice, he selected one that was dyed in sunset hues—destined for the third-story guest bedroom overlooking the street.

"I'm glad we got that out of the way," he said, taking the bag from the vendor.

"Anyone else you need to buy gifts for?" Toni asked.

"Perhaps a shot glass for my son's collection."

David joined them with a large packet of fish, and they meandered through the rest of the market before heading down a well-worn boulevard interspersed with modern storefronts flaunting design brands for everything from perfume to sunglasses.

At the wine store, Rex paid for two bottles of Saint-Émilion as his contribution to the dinner. Then, carrying the groceries between them, he and David found the limo parked up the side street from the café where Pascal awaited them. As Toni left to fetch him, Rex set the bags on the sidewalk by the trunk of the car.

"Dave, you knew Sabine from before, didn't you?" he ventured, knowing full well that he had, according to the Winslows.

"She waited tables at my restaurant years before I opened the cordon bleu school. That was when she was still a struggling actress. She lived in Paris but was schooled in England. Being bi-lingual helped no end. She could turn the French accent on for the clients and she knew her wines, which was a great asset."

"Did you get to know her well?" Rex hoped the question did not come across as indiscreet as it sounded.

"Well enough. Toni worked at the restaurant at the time, and they sometimes didn't see eye to eye, but nothing beyond the usual that goes on in a restaurant. Sabine met our old friends, the Winslows, there and they ended up letting her the flat in their basement. Eventually, she went on to bigger and better things."

"Met Vernon."

"That's right. Her star was already set, but there's no doubt he made things happen more quickly for her. In fact, she was on holiday here at La Plage with the Winslows one summer while Vernon was here with his first wife. They ran into each other a few years later in New York. Vernon was divorced by then."

"Elizabeth told me she didn't approve of the match."

"Did she?" David Weeks pondered this fact. "I thought Vernon was quite a catch. Rich, lots of connections in the entertainment business. But women see these things a bit differently, don't they?"

"There was the age difference to consider."

"I suppose, but some women like older men. Sabine was estranged from her dad, a rich banker who didn't approve of her acting aspirations. Maybe she was looking for a father figure. And Vernon is in great shape for his age."

"Did you ever meet Sabine's parents?"

"Don't recall that I did. Her family is from the stuffy *sixième arrondissement* in Paris. That's about all I know. Elizabeth and Paul were like surrogate parents." David glanced at his watch. "Where did Toni get to, I wonder?"

At that moment, his wife turned the street corner with Pascal in tow. "Sorry to keep you waiting. I had a quick Porto at the café."

"Nice for *you*," David grumbled. "We're dying of heat stroke and thirst out here after lugging all the shopping."

"We have drinks in da car, don' you worry, Mr. Weeks," the driver assured him, unlocking the door.

"Just as bloody well." David stared pointedly at his wife as she got in, but she seemed unruffled. She even winked becomingly at Rex who piled in after her.

"What do you plan to do for the rest of the day?" she asked as they relaxed in the air-conditioned comfort of the limo headed back to La Plage.

"I thought I'd explore the far end of the beach and find a quiet bar to write my postcards."

"Try The Sand Bar," David recommended, happier now that he had a beer in his hand. "There's a shaded spot up on the wooden terrace, and the rum drinks are cheaper than anywhere else."

"Aye, well I don't intend to drink too many of those. I need to work on the case this afternoon."

"Well, don't work too hard," Toni said. "Tonight's supposed to lighten the mood for those of us who came out here for a holiday."

The inference was that she'd had enough of the gloom surrounding Sabine's disappearance. Clearly, from everything she had said and written on the subject, not much love had been lost between the two women.

After helping Pascal and David take the groceries to the Weeks' front door, Rex made a detour to his cabana before setting out for The Sand Bar, equipped with his postcards and note pad, and everything else he might need for an afternoon at the beach. He still had to figure out a way to outsmart that fox Bijou, but it was hard to do when the fox was in his own territory and had all the loopholes covered and the police held at bay.

By the time he left for the Weeks' barbecue that evening, freshly showered and dressed for the occasion, he had not made much progress in the case. The potent daiquiris at The Sand Bar, added to the various distractions afforded by the screaming hordes on the banana boat and other water sports in the bay, had not been conducive to achieving a whole lot of thinking.

A breeze stirred the fronds in the palm trees, agitating the Chinese lanterns, still unlit. The sobbing wail of a saxophone vibrated through the sultry air, emanating from a CD player at the Weeks' eighth and final cabana. The guests in pareos and wraps gathered on the patio, sipping tall drinks decorated with straws and miniumbrellas, while Gaby, long blond hair flowing down her bare back, offered him a plate of pumpernickel squares topped with smoked salmon. As he thanked her in Latin, he spotted Mrs. Winslow in her flame-colored sarong and the Greek necklace with the interlocking wave motif.

"You're staring at me. I must look especially ravishing tonight," she joked.

"That you do." He led her aside. "There's also something bothering me. I hope you can clear it up."

Elizabeth stared at him with stricken eyes. "I'll try."

"It concerns a photo of you taken by Vernon the night of Sabine's disappearance."

"At the party? People were taking pictures all night. It was just us, and Hastings didn't object. He must have decided to bend the rules for Paul's birthday. But I honestly can't remember. We were all quite blotto."

"That must be it," Rex said. "But Vernon swears he didn't have his camera phone that night."

"Perhaps someone picked it up by mistake. Is it important?"

"It was found by the rocks."

"Maybe Vernon dropped it. How do you know you can believe him?"

"I don't." Rex gazed around the patio, taking in all the guests. How did he know he could believe any of them?

Brooklyn was conspicuous by his absence. Rex inquired after him, not having seen him all day.

"Dropped us like a hot brick," David complained, manipulating the fish fillets on the barbecue. "Makes me think Sabine was the only reason he hung around in the first place. One summer he brought a girl. Just the one time, mind you."

"Maybe he's got someone in Philipsburg," Pam said. "That's where he spends all his time. I haven't seen his cute butt on the beach in over a week."

"He's in mourning for Sabine," Sean O'Sullivan warbled, already four sheets to the wind.

Nora silenced him with a glare. "Will you listen to him prattling on?" she said to the company at large, eyes flitting toward Vernon who sat morosely in a corner.

"Brook flew back to the States," Paul Winslow informed everyone. "He'll be back Wednesday."

That was news to Rex.

"He had to put out a fire on Wall Street. Loss of investor confidence in some company or other."

Rex flopped back in his chair.

"Don't look so put out, old chap." Winslow handed him a whiskey on the rocks. "He said he had to leave in a hurry to avoid a tropical depression that's moving in from the south. I hate to think of that plane of his being buffeted around like a shuttlecock over the ocean. I told him to get going before it was too late."

Rex wondered what incentive Brooklyn could possibly have to return if it was in fact true that Sabine had been his primary reason for being at La Plage. Thinking of love interests, he remembered he was meeting Helen off the ship in Philipsburg on Monday and arranged with Paul for the loan of his Jeep.

"By the way, Paul, do you know a night club down there called The Stiletto?"

"I don't, but Duke might. He knows all the joints in Philipsburg."

The Texan turned toward them, puffing on a fat Cuban cigar. "Do I feel my ears burnin'?"

"Rex was inquiring about The Stiletto in Philipsburg."

"Haven't been in a coupla years, not since that business with one of the dancers getting murdered. Poor kid. They found her mutilated body in a cellar."

"Do you remember her?" Rex asked.

"Sure do. Face like an angel, body like a whore. What a combination." Farley stuck the cigar in his mouth.

"Has this anything to do with our case?" Winslow asked Rex.

"It might, but Bijou was at his club the night Sabine went missing. I have witnesses attesting to that fact."

"Reliable?"

"The bar manager and the accountant, both of whom confirmed having a meeting with him."

"Bijou took me there with Pam once," the Texan told Rex. "This was when he was looking for investors for his club-casino in Marigot. Said he was scouting out the best dancers on the island. He bought out The Stiletto at around that time."

"Do you know if he was personally acquainted with Leona Couch?"

Duke Farley prodded his malodorous cigar in Rex's direction. "Leona. That was her name. He was fascinated by her. When she did her routine, he looked like his borehole had yielded a shitload of oil."

Rex pulled his pipe from his pocket and pensively thumbed Clan tobacco into the bowl. He found he resorted less to his habit in hot weather, but the mellow-sweet fragrance went some way to counteracting the cigar smoke polluting the storm-expectant air. Finally, under the pretext of getting another drink, he moved away from Farley and sought out Sean O'Sullivan, eager to probe him for more information on the Jewel Killings before further drink rendered the Irishman senseless.

In spite of Bijou's alibi in the Durand case, he wanted to see if he could pin the other girls' murders on him and make it stick. Too much smoke existed for there not to be a fire somewhere.

FOURTEEN

When Rex returned to his cabana later that night, he eased open Brooklyn's door and was reassured to see his personal items lying about the room. It wasn't simply that he would feel slighted had Brooklyn just taken off without saying goodbye; Rex had realized when he first heard of his departure that he genuinely liked and admired the man. He was courageous, intelligent, and successful, and yet for all that, appeared to be someone who would lend an ear in time of trouble and extend a hand in time of need.

He sincerely hoped he was not wrong about Brooklyn.

The next morning he awoke dehydrated from a hangover and found the room darker than usual, even at this advanced hour. A rainstorm had knocked the frond of a coconut palm against the cabana roof all night, and now a blustery day greeted him when he stepped onto the patio.

A tornado-shaped cloud loomed on the horizon. The last sailboat had disappeared from the bay, presumably to find a safer haven. The yellow umbrellas stood furled on the sand, contributing to the desolate scene. Since it was not beach weather, Rex decided to spend part of the day canvassing the nearby tourist spots, starting with the Sundown Ranch.

"'The Rundown Ranch,' as Sabine and I jokingly called it," Brooklyn had confided the other day when he gave Rex a photo of the two of them standing by a paddock fence.

After the recent storm, the gully-washed road proved more hazardous than usual, and he made slow progress to the ranch, where the photo elicited an almost hysterical response from the owner. *Mon Dieu!* She knew Mademoiselle Sabine very well, always personally made sure Dancer was available and fresh for her ride. *Quelle horreur!* To think such an atrocity had happened not two miles from here! Theft, yes, that happened from time to time. Just two weeks ago, the dispensary in the stable had been broken into and some potent drugs stolen. "*Des drogués,*" she announced, making her eyes go spacey in imitation of a drug addict. They did not care what they put in their bodies, these young people.

She shook her head sorrowfully at the photograph. "*Ah, le pauvre!*" she exclaimed, referring to Brooklyn. The two lovebirds had been so close. How he must miss her . . .

Tapping the photo against the palm of his hand, Rex stepped back through the mud to the Jeep. A young woman unsaddled a horse steaming from its recent exercise and hosed it down in the yard. He removed his sandals as he got in the car and placed them upside down on the passenger mat. Barefoot, he drove out through the broken-down gate, leaving behind the smell of wet hay and manure, and proceeded along Le Galion Beach Road until he came to a large meshed structure with a sign advertising the Butterfly Farm.

After paying his admission and declining the guided tour, he entered the net enclosure. Serenaded by the melodic Enya floating down from the speakers, he ambled through a giant terrarium harboring hundreds of butterfly species from Saba, Cambodia, Trinidad, Indonesia, China, and elsewhere, meandering among the flowering plants in the soothing green shade. A Monarch alighted on his shoulder.

"It may be attracted to your aftershave," the guide remarked before turning back to her group of visitors and describing how certain butterflies mated for thirty-six hours out of their two-week life-span.

Rex wondered if that was proportionate to human adult sexual activity and, based on his own experience, decided it wasn't; butterflies definitely fared better in that department. When the mating was disturbed, the guide went on to explain, they flew away together, the female carrying the male. This drew laughs from the crowd. He overheard, too, that the farm had been the brainchild of two eccentric Englishmen, which really didn't surprise him. The English had the market cornered on quaintness.

The serene butterfly surroundings exerted a calming influence upon him and he lingered longer than he had intended, studying the pupae that resembled exquisite designer earrings and following the trail of a stately red peacock with black markings and a large purple and yellow eyespot on the tip of each wing.

Making sure no insects had adhered to his clothing, he exited the screened door and stepped back into the souvenir store.

"Can you tell me if you recognize this couple?" he asked the middle-aged woman at the counter, showing her the snapshot of Brooklyn and Sabine.

"Well, I recognize her," the store clerk said in a broad English accent. "She's the missing actress, Sabine Duras."

"Durand."

"Are you a reporter?" she asked in a forthright manner.

"No, I'm a friend of a friend hoping to locate her."

"She was here two or three times, but I don't know the man in the photo—I'd remember such a hunky bloke. Not that the man with her wasn't attractive too."

"Do you remember his nationality?" His heart raced in excitement.

"The first time I saw them, they requested a French-speaking guide, but she spoke English with me. She autographed one of our brochures. She's even lovelier in real life."

"What did her friend look like?"

"Medium height, dark hair, sexy smile. About her age, maybe younger. He wore those wraparound sunglasses and never took them off, so I didn't get a chance to look at his eyes. He seemed a bit twitchy."

"Twitchy?"

"Sort of nervous. Kept looking around. Maybe he was worried about the paparazzi, but St. Martin is really very low key and we tend to respect people's privacy here."

"When did they come in last?"

"Two weeks ago, maybe. Monday, I think it was. That's right. She asked about a framed display of a striped moth. We didn't have it so I ordered one for the shop. Here's the entry," the store clerk said. "July ninth."

Sabine had disappeared the next day. As Rex headed back toward the resort for lunch, he wondered about this new man in her life. Where could he find him? Was he connected to Bijou in some way?

Pale grey clouds mottled the sky, threatening rain. His thoughts diverted to Helen. Hopefully the weather would clear up by tomorrow in time for her visit. He recalled how they had watched the swans on the lake in Sussex, how she had played footsie with him that night in his bed. They had exchanged cards and e-mails since Christmas, had spoken a few times on the phone, but there had been a certain reticence in their conversations. He could not be sure if she was still dating the mathematics teacher at the school where she was a student counselor. And, of course, Moira had been in the picture, so there could be no question of taking the relationship further.

Now that his conscience was clear with regard to Moira Wilcox, he looked forward to Helen's visit as much as a mooning teenager on his first date.

FIFTEEN

A WHITE, MULTI-TIERED FLOATING hotel docked on Great Bay overshadowed the boats ferrying passengers to port. The yellow funnel emblazoned with "Fun-Sun" in blue letters assured Rex this was indeed Helen's ship. But where was she?

Suddenly he spotted her through the crowd milling by the terminal. "Helen!" he shouted, cupping his hands to his mouth and waving frantically.

She half-ran toward him, a smile breaking out on her face. Her nautical style navy and white dress fit her just right. Her tanned skin brought out the blue of her eyes, and she had done something with her hair—he couldn't tell what, but it seemed softer than he remembered.

"You look wonderful," he told her, deliberating whether to embrace her, and suddenly wanting to very much.

"And you look very huggable." She stood on her toes in her mid-heel sandals and flung her arms around his shoulders. "Do I get a kiss?"

Gathering her in his arms, he kissed her full on the lips.

"Do you notice anything about me?"

Rex panicked. Such a question from a woman always inspired him with dread. Had she lost weight? "You did something with your hair?" he asked hopefully.

"I'm wearing the earrings!"

"So you are." The tiny turquoise-studded swans he had bought for her in Swanmere Village dangled from her ears.

"I didn't notice them at first because your hair sort of covers them. It looks very nice, by the way. Very soft and wavy."

She smiled, and he felt pleased with himself at making such an adroit comeback.

"Honey-chile," a black mama called out from a folding chair located beside a crate of beads. "Lemme give you some braids."

"Maybe later," Helen replied. "Only a dollar a braid," she told Rex wistfully.

Never able to understand the compulsion women had for changing their hairstyles, he took her hand and drew her away. They passed the duty-free shops and discount stores on Front Street where merchants stood at their posts bracing for the onslaught of bargain-seekers let loose from the cruise.

"I can't believe the price of clothes and electronic goods here," Helen exclaimed. "And look at those watches."

In a pharmacy, Rex spotted tortoiseshell compacts like the one he had seen in Nora O'Sullivan's possession. Perhaps Sabine had bought hers in here too.

"It's very much like St. Thomas," Helen said. "I got this gold bracelet there." She shook the gold chain on her wrist.

"Are you sure it's real?"

"I'll get it appraised when I get home. Anyway, I like it." She stopped to gaze at a window display of blue Delft from Holland. "I should get some linen napkins since they're so cheap. Everything's tax-free as well."

Rex found a seat inside the store and waited patiently until, holding a small bag of purchases, Helen led him back onto the street.

"Oh, look, the Guavaberry Emporium. I read about it in the brochure. We can try some for free."

They sampled the sweet liqueur at the counter. Helen opted to buy an opaque green bottle of banana rum instead.

"Can we get lunch now?" Rex asked.

"If we must. All we've been doing on the ship is eating. I think some people go on cruises just for the food, judging by the size of the passengers."

"Well, I haven't eaten since my *pain au chocolat* this morning. And I'm dying for a beer."

They settled for an outdoor table at a dockside café and ordered drinks and seafood platters.

"You don't look like you got a lot of sun during your week out here," Helen observed.

"A tan makes my freckles stand out. Anyway, we had a bit of rain over the weekend—but it's cleared up nicely." He looked up in appreciation at the cloudless blue sky.

"Are you having a good time?" she asked.

"Except when I'm reminded what a polyglot I'm not."

"A polyglot?"

"Someone who speaks many languages. My German is passable, but my French seems to afford much mirth to anyone within earshot. It's verra embarrassing."

Helen laughed. "Your Scots accent must sound funny in French. I can't wait to hear you speak it."

"Not a chance."

Helen chuckled into her glass of white wine. "I suppose the word 'polyglot' is Latin?"

"No, it's from the Greek."

"Rex, you really need to get out more."

"I'm here, aren't I?" He extended his arms to indicate their exotic surroundings. "Hobnobbing with the jet set."

"Well, I admit you're less uptight than when I first met you. A bit of sun can do wonders. You look totally different in casual clothes."

Rex may have looked casual, but there was nothing casual about the way he had tried on five shirts that morning in an effort to look as appealing as possible for Helen's benefit. He had finally settled on a short-sleeved, loose-fitting button-down shirt worn over khaki shorts reaching his knees and equipped with so many pockets he was convinced he would forget in which one he'd placed the car keys.

"I bought these clothes in Miami, down to the designer leather flip-flops, which Campbell assured me were worth the extra forty dollars—even though I couldna tell the difference from the no-name brands."

"You look very nice. And very authentic," Helen added. "Campbell has good taste."

"If 'good' equates to 'expensive,' I can assure you he does that. I remember when I was a student, the only clothes manufacturers' names we knew were Wrangler and Levi."

"Life was simpler then."

"Aye, and you didn't need a degree in advanced technology to make a phone call."

"You old dinosaur."

She said it in such a fond way that he suddenly liked the idea of being an old dinosaur. Well, not *old* exactly, but a seasoned, warrior dinosaur. He relaxed in his chair with a contented sigh and signaled to the passing waiter for another beer and white wine for Helen. "This is a grand place to be."

"It certainly is. So, have you heard from your girlfriend yet?"

"Aye, well, there's been a development."

As they tackled their seafood, he told her about Moira's desertion and how he felt like a fool after making all those inquiries over the phone to her hotel and to the British Embassy in Baghdad. "She could have told me sooner and spared me all the trouble," he concluded.

"She was probably embarrassed."

"As well she should be."

"So do I get to see where you're staying now that you're a free man?"

"If you'd like. It's at the other end of the island but we can get there in half an hour. I better warn you, though—it's a nudist resort."

"No! Are you having me on? I just can't picture you in that sort of place."

"I keep my swimming trunks on," Rex said modestly.

Helen suppressed a giggle. "This I've got to see." She wiped a tear of laughter from her eye.

"I'm not as much of a prude as all that, you know. Isn't that what you called me back at Swanmere?"

"I did," Helen said, recovering slowly. "So, do you interview all these people in the never-never?" She chuckled again.

"Mostly, but it's strange how quickly you get used to it. After a few days, you hardly notice at all."

"Well, I'm jealous. The thought of you ogling naked young women all day..."

"There's no need for jealousy. Most aren't that young." He raised his glass. "I only have eyes for you!"

"Flatterer." She mouthed him a kiss across the table. "So how is Campbell getting on in Florida?"

"He finished his first year with a 3.5 grade point average, out of a possible 4, so I'm quite pleased."

"Good for him."

"Aye, well he's making a point, trying to prove I was wrong in not wanting him to go there in the first place." Rex thumbed his glass. "It's hard when they move away from home, but it's interesting seeing him grow into his own person. He's not really like me at all."

"Is that good or bad?"

"Who knows? And my mother's getting on. I don't know how long she'll be around."

"Rex, you sound lonely!"

"Well, now that Moira's run off, I'm feeling quite abandoned. I'm glad you came, Helen, I truly am."

"It's not just a question of being on the rebound, is it?"

"Definitely not! To tell the truth, I'm glad it turned out this way. I always felt an attraction for you, lass. I really enjoy being with you."

"Likewise—well, you know how I feel about you." Helen tipped the rest of her wine in her mouth and slid her purse strap over her shoulder. "How about some sightseeing?"

"What, you mean *now?*" He wanted to spend some personal time with her.

"Just a little foray into the Sint Maarten Museum."

He must have looked less than enthused as he hurriedly paid the bill.

"A bit of culture, Rex. Did you know, the island's first settlers, the Arawaks…"

Rex, only half paying attention, concentrated on finding the museum, which was hidden down an alleyway. The converted nineteenth-century dwelling held an archived collection of sepia photos of hurricanes and an assortment of musketry, blackened cookware, and other island memorabilia.

"I love all these old artifacts, seeing how people lived back in the olden days," Helen said, peering into a glass display. "Oh, look at these funny misshapen cannon balls."

"Aye," Rex said absent-mindedly, more interested in a model ship of *The Fair Rosamund*, a slave vessel depicted as stealing away with human cargo onboard. A diagram showed how the captives were packed like sardines in the hold. An absolute disgrace, he thought.

"What now?" he asked hopefully when they had seen everything the small museum had to offer.

"I really would like to see where you're staying. We still have bags of time."

"You'll like the beach."

"I've seen plenty of beaches. I want to see more of you." She raised an eyebrow in unmistakable wickedness.

Rex cleared his throat. "My chariot awaits."

He escorted her to Paul's beat-up safari-style Jeep and stowed her purchases on the back seat. Pulling out of the parking space, he proceeded to give a potted history of the island. "Philipsburg was founded in 1763 by John Philips, a Scottish captain in the Dutch navy," he announced proudly.

"Those intrepid Scots," Helen said, smiling at him.

Rex took the most direct route back to the northeast side of St. Martin and they arrived at the resort in good time. Leaving the jeep outside his cabana, he ushered Helen inside before they could be accosted by a nude guest. He flipped the sign to "*Do Not Disturb.*"

"Where's the roommate you were telling me about?" Helen asked.

"In New York. Fortunately for us. Or, should I say, for me. If you met him, you'd forget all about yours truly."

"Now, why would you say that? Is he very good-looking?"

"Aye. He even races his own cars and flies his own plane."

Helen laughed. "Ah, well. I suppose I'll just have to do with you then, won't I?"

"Ta verra much."

She planted a kiss on his mouth. "Can I see your room now?"

Rex swept open the bedroom door. A dozen dewy red roses stood in a vase by the bedside, per his instructions to the front desk that morning.

"Oh, these smell divine," Helen exclaimed, bending over the arrangement. "Are they for me?"

"What d'ye think! Your name's on the card."

Helen drew the tiny envelope from the bouquet and opened it. She spoke the words aloud:

> *'O, my Luve's like a red, red rose*
> *sweetly play'd in tune.*

Rex continued the poem from memory.

> *'As fair art thou, my bonnie lass,*
> *So deep in luve am I;*
> *And I will luve thee still, my dear,*
> *Till a' the seas gang dry.*
>
> *Till a' the seas gang dry, my dear,*
> *And the rocks melt wi' the sun:*
> *I will luve thee still, my dear,*
> *While the sands o' life shall run.*
>
> *And fare thee weel, my only Luve!*
> *And fare thee weel a while!*
> *And I will come again, my Luve,*
> *Tho' it ware ten thousand mile!*

"Oh, Rex, that is so romantic."

He bowed. "It's by Robbie Burns."

"I love that poem. How clever of you to be able to recite it so flawlessly."

"It's my party piece. It's also the only poem I know." He hoped Helen was not going to read too much into it.

She clasped her hands around his neck and kissed him. Rex returned the kiss with fervor. Turning around, she lifted her hair so he could unzip her dress, which he obligingly did, and a minute later, she stood before him in her lacy bra and panties, bronzed and nicely proportioned.

"Well, don't just stand there all gormless-like," she teased in an exaggerated northern English dialect.

"I'm just admiring."

She unbuckled his belt while he attended to the buttons on his shirt. "I always wanted to look under a Scotsman's kilt," she confessed.

"I hope I do Bonny Scotland proud," he said stepping out of his boxers.

"Oh, you certainly do, Rex," Helen said happily.

SIXTEEN

"I WISH I COULD stay here," Helen said stretching beside him in the king-size bed. Her face looked as fresh as the roses on the bedside table, her eyes clear and bright. Rex felt pretty good himself.

Glancing at the alarm clock, she gave a sigh. "I suppose I'd better get up and take a quick shower."

Rex lazed in bed, listening to the water running in the next room. A pity she had to leave so soon. Already he began fantasizing about all the missed opportunities between now and when he would see her again. In the meantime, he had an obligation to the Winslows to fulfill.

"Is there anything to drink?" Helen asked, returning to the room with her hair wrapped in a turban. "I worked up quite a thirst!"

"Shameless lass," he said throwing off the rumpled covers. "There's some banana rum. It's verra refreshing with ice."

"That would be perfect. Lots of ice."

Rex followed her into the living room. She walked starkers onto the patio, toweling her hair dry. Rex appreciated the fact that she felt natural about her nudity, but was embarrassed what the guests might think about him bringing a woman back to the resort for some afternoon delight. They might think he had picked her up on the beach. *Oh, tae heck with it*, he thought. The Weeks waved from the beach. Helen gave an enthusiastic wave back.

"Don't encourage them. We only have a wee bit of time left to ourselves."

"Who are they?" she asked, taking her drink from him.

"David and Toni. They own a cookery school in Richmond."

"Cheers." Helen clinked his glass. "To many more consummations."

"Many more." He tapped her pert nose. "We best get going if we don't want to rush."

Ten minutes later, he opened the door of the Jeep, and she slid inside. As he drove toward Philipsburg, he couldn't take his eyes off her tanned knees, covered in a fine down of golden hair.

"How is the case going?" she asked.

"Slowly. The evidence conveniently points to the husband, but it's all circumstantial. His phone was found at the scene. He was the last person to appear at the restaurant where the guests were gathered for a birthday party. He suspected his wife was having an affair with my millionaire playboy roommate, and there are witnesses to the husband physically abusing her."

"Sabine Durand, the actress."

"You've heard of her?"

"Even the British tabloids have got hold of her now."

"They must be more cultured than I thought."

"Only because she disappeared. They are drawing comparisons between your case and Natalee Holloway, who went missing on

Aruba." Helen shook her head sadly. "Imagine a mother never knowing for sure what happened to her daughter."

"It's hardly my case, as you call it. I feel like a third wheel. But since no body has been found, the authorities aren't proceeding further with the investigation. All I can do is get a bit closer to the truth of what happened."

"You're good at that. You found out who was responsible for the murders at Swanmere Manor. It makes sense the new owners of the hotel would have thought of you when their friend vanished."

"I don't know if this case will ever be closed. If the sharks got to her, there's little chance of finding her remains and performing an autopsy."

"I have absolute faith in you."

"I appreciate the sentiment, Helen, but dinna jinx it." He checked the map on the dashboard to make sure he was still on the right road.

"I expect a tourist leaked news of Sabine's disappearance to the British press," Helen said. "Mostly it's speculation."

"It's amazing what passes for news these days." He had watched CNN in his Miami hotel room on the way to the Caribbean and been disconcerted to find more discussion about celebrities than information on world affairs.

"A pretty young woman going missing raises a lot of conjecture. Any other suspects?" Helen asked.

"Well, I thought I might be on to something. I went to check out a night club which is owned by a certain Monsieur Bijou."

"Mr. Jewel. Is that his real name?"

"Not exactly. He's a Dutch national by the name of Coenraad van Bijhooven."

"No wonder he changed it. What did you find out?"

"Only that he has an alibi for the night Ms. Durand disappeared, which is more than can be said for most of the guests at the resort. The manager at The Stiletto has a dated surveillance tape of him getting out of his chauffeur-driven car and parading through the doors in a white suit at 5:55 p.m. for a meeting with the accountant. I called the accountant to confirm the meeting."

"Could Bijou have sent someone to the resort to do his dirty work for him?"

"From what I understand, Bijou likes to do his own dirty work. And it would have been hard to conduct an abduction at the beach. The spot is somewhat inaccessible and there's a chance of being heard." Rex pumped the steering wheel in frustration. "There are so many things that don't add up."

"Like what?"

"She was supposedly seeing a chiropractor, but the number was bogus."

"Perhaps someone took it down wrong."

"I doubt it. The receptionist is right efficient. And I couldn't find a Dr. Sganarelle listed anywhere on the island."

"It is an unusual name. It's a character out of a play by Molière."

"Really? The eighteenth-century French playwright?"

"Seventeenth century."

"What sort of character?" Rex asked.

"He's a possessive miser who doesn't want to part with his daughter's dowry, so he prevents her from having suitors and leaving the house. When she becomes 'lovesick,' her secret admirer pretends to be a doctor so he can see her, and he prescribes a staged wedding as a cure. Since the wedding turns out to be legally binding, the old man is tricked into marrying off his daughter. It was a corny play, but I had to study it for French 'A' level."

"What was the doctor imposter's name?"

"Um, let me see…" Helen stared out of the window at the passing countryside. "Cle-, no, Clitandre. That sounds too literary by half."

Rex swerved and brought the car to a standstill on the grass verge.

"What's the matter?" Helen asked. "Do we have a flat?"

"You truly are a multi-faceted woman, Helen," he murmured, turning to face her.

"Why, thank you. Are you merely referring to my cultural knowledge?"

He caught the look of mischief in her blue eyes. "Aye," he said, caressing her knee. "That too."

"If you hadn't been such a prig, I could have spent a whole week with you here, instead of with a bunch of teachers from my school."

"You said the cruise has been fun."

"Well, yes, it has. But I see them almost every day at work."

"Is Clive on the cruise?"

"No," Helen said primly. "He doesn't like hot weather. And, anyway, I told you I finished with him."

"He's probably sobbing into his logarithms right now."

"Now, don't be mean, Rex. He wasn't as boring as you like to make out."

"Are you trying to make me jealous?"

"Are you jealous?"

"Yes, but you have about ten minutes to reassure me until we have to get going to catch your ship." He bent toward her and kissed her.

"It can leave without me for all I care," she told him, tilting back her seat. "Couldn't you have found something bigger than this Jeep? What if someone sees us?"

Rex slid his hand up her smooth thigh. "There may be a few voyeuristic goats."

"Oh, well, I'm sure they've seen it all before. After all, we're still on the French side."

She reached for his belt while he pushed her dress up her hips. Somehow he managed to clamber over the console. Suddenly, he heard a car engine drop to second gear as it negotiated the road up the hill. He glanced through the back window of the Jeep.

"Watch out," he said, struggling back into his seat.

Panting and perspiring, they managed to regain their sitting positions and straighten their clothes before the police car drew up alongside their stationary Jeep. Lieutenant Latour's mustachioed face appeared at the window.

Rex lowered it, discombobulated but relieved he'd not been caught with his pants down.

"*Ah, Monsieur Graves. Quelle coincidence. Vous avez besoin d'aide?*"

No, we don't need your blasted help. "Merci, voozette gentil mais nous sommes trez biens," Rex gushed, reassuring him they were fine.

"*Ça se voit!*" the officer said with a leering glint in his eye. "So I see!"

"*Nous étions en panne,*" Helen interjected. "*Mais nous avons réussi à changer le pneu. Quelle chaleur!*" she said, wiping her brow as if from the exertion of having just changed a tire.

"*Madame parle très bien le français!*" Latour complimented her on her French. He winked at Rex and twiddled his mustache. "*Elle est charmante!*"

"*Noo sommes en retard por le bateau.* The boat." Rex frantically pointed to his watch. "*A bientôt! Merci!*" He thrust the jeep into gear and tore off down the road with a squeal of tires.

"What was all that about?" Helen asked.

"He's the gendarme I've been liaising with in the Sabine Durand case."

Helen gave a hoot of laughter. "Of all the cars on all the roads on St. Martin, he walks up to mine?"

"Something like that. Still, it's not a verra big island. Ach! If I had any credibility to begin with, I've lost it now."

Helen started giggling. It was a good few minutes before she regained control of herself. "Your—your French," she gasped. "It's *épouvantable!*"

"Didn't I warn you? Thanks for coming up with the story about the car breaking down. Not that I think he believed us for a minute."

"He seemed quite *gallant* though."

"I'd like to have wiped that smirk off his face. Mind you," Rex said thoughtfully, remembering Latour leaving the house in Grand Case with his own clothes in a state of disarray, "I don't think he's in any position to cast stones."

Although he resented the interruption to their romantic interlude, the episode grew increasingly funny as they embellished it on the way to Philipsburg, where they had difficulty finding a parking space. Shiploads of marauding tourists inundated the narrow streets of the port. Wives loaded beleaguered husbands with battery-operated electronic devices, apparel, sandals, and all sorts of condiments and ornaments symbolic of the Caribbean.

"Here, luv, can you manage this lot?" said one. "We still have to get rum for Kevin. And Tracy wanted one of them shell thingamybobs to hang in her bedroom."

Helen hailed a fellow passenger. "Laura, could you take our picture?" She handed the lady her digital camera and stood against Rex, who draped his arm around her waist. "Thanks, Laura." Helen checked the picture in the frame. "Wait a sec and I'll help you with those bags."

The woman stood by while Helen and Rex embraced.

"I'll e-mail you the photo," Helen promised him.

"'Fare thee weel!' Enjoy St. Kitts."

"The rest of the cruise will pale in comparison with the time spent with you."

"Aye, it was grand, wasn't it?"

The friend smiled sympathetically at Rex and gave one of her souvenir bags to Helen to carry. They moved away, Helen glancing back over her shoulder before finally disappearing among the throng of embarking passengers.

This parting was less painful than the last one, Rex reflected. There would be other times, he felt sure of that now. He would call her as soon as he returned to Edinburgh and then drive down to Derby to see her. Consoled by that thought, he went off in search of a beer and came back half an hour later, by which time the dock had drained like a bottle. Only a spatter of people remained.

Helen, a blur behind the white deck rail of the cruise ship, waved and pointed at him to two women who stood beside her—presumably teachers in her group. As he waved her off from the ferry terminal, he hoped he created a good impression.

The Full Moon Party at the end of the month would have made for a special evening with Helen, if he himself was still around. He hoped to have solved the case by then and be on his way back home.

SEVENTEEN

"WHO'S THE PETITE BLONDE I saw you with yesterday?" Weeks asked Rex as they met on the path leading to the cabanas.

"A friend from home. She came over on a cruise."

"When are we going to meet her?"

"She had to get back to the ship."

"Pity. We could use some new blood in the group. Tensions are running a bit high. All the stress over Sabine, I suppose. Anyway, it's not the same." David Weeks glanced at the paper bag in Rex's hand. "I see you got yourself some breakfast. I was just on my way to the pâtisserie myself."

Rex watched his retreating tanned backside. He had gotten used to nudity on the beach, but it still struck him as strange that the guests wandered into the store to buy groceries with not so much as a stitch on their bodies.

"Rex! Rex!" a male voice halted him from the parking lot.

He turned and saw the doctor and his family descending from the limo.

"My daughter Gaby needs to speak with you most urgently."

Rex approached her. "What is it, lass?"

Gaby handed him a photograph from a packet of processed film. "Who do you think that is?" she asked hesitantly while he studied it.

"It looks like Sabine Durand, judging by other photos I've seen of her. Though it's a wee bit difficult to be sure because of the sunglasses."

"They are her Christian Dior glasses," Frau von Mueller said.

Rex failed to understand why they were showing him a snapshot of the actress when he already knew what she looked like.

"I took it yesterday," Gaby informed him.

"What?" How was that possible, unless... "Where?"

"On St. Barthélemy," the mother garbled in excitement. "Gaby went to buy a new snorkel mask. She heard the voice of Sabine at the café next door to the shop *und* she snapped the picture."

"I couldn't be sure at first," Gaby took over, "because—well, I thought she was dead. I was able to take this picture without her seeing me. I had the pictures developed in town."

"It is her," the doctor insisted. "I would know the nose anywhere. I made it!"

"Who else knows about this?" Rex asked.

"No one," Gaby said. "First I wanted to be sure and examine the photograph. Here is the address of the dive store," she added, giving him the receipt from the purchase of her mask.

"She is going to be a fine lawyer, *nein?*" von Mueller said proudly.

"Aye, she acted verra correctly."

The girl blushed to her flaxen roots.

"Can I keep this photo for the moment?" Rex checked his watch and flagged down the limo, automatically patting down the pockets of his shorts to make sure he had his wallet on him. "Not a word to anyone!" he called back to the von Mueller family, putting a finger to his lips.

Pascal rolled down the window. "Yessir, Mr. Graves?"

"I need to get to Oyster Pond by nine o'clock."

"Hop in."

Rex tore around the sleek black hood of the limo and settled in beside the driver. "Go as fast as you can," he instructed.

Pascal handled the stretch limo like a race car pro as vehicles and pedestrians prudently leaped out of their path. Rex offered him one of his croissants and wolfed down the other. At Oyster Pond, dockhands were already casting off the lines of the large twin-hulled ferry. Rex waved frantically, thrust his fare and his I.D. at the woman behind the kiosk, and jumped aboard.

Thankful he'd had a bit of breakfast to help settle his stomach, he stood on the top deck while the high-speed catamaran set motor sail over a choppy sea. He took a few precautionary gulps of air and stared straight ahead at the gray-green mirage of St. Barts to the southwest. The memory of the slave vessel slipping away from the island sprang to mind as the coast of St. Martin receded. Now that Sabine had been spotted, he suspected her of acting out the affair with Brooklyn and giving her husband a motive for murder, and then making her exit by sea. Had she planted his phone on the beach? If so, why was Elizabeth Winslow on the camera? He was in no doubt whose face it was in the frame. The outline of the necklace she always wore was clearly visible. Had Mrs. Winslow aided Sabine in her plan? Why then had she and her husband

149

brought him to St. Martin to investigate the young woman's disappearance?

Already the sun bounced blindingly off the water. Rex found a stick of sunscreen in his pocket and smeared it over his face. The deck hand served plastic cups of guava juice to the passengers, and Rex downed one thirstily. He glanced with impatience between his watch and St. Barts growing progressively clearer in focus.

He had until four-thirty to find the actress. That was when the catamaran left for Oyster Pond. The island of St. Barts was small, no more that ten square miles. How many hotels could be on it? He wondered if he should enlist the help of the local gendarmes. Yet, if it was indeed Sabine in the photo, no murder had taken place after all. Ms. Durand was a grown woman, and if she had chosen to take off on her vacation without alerting her husband, the police would not be inclined to go after her.

A family of tourists pointed overboard in excitement. A green sea turtle paddled alongside the boat. Rex wished he had brought his camera, but he'd left in a rush. Gustavia Harbor came into view, a small port bristling with masts from the fleet of fishing and leisure craft. A small red-roofed town grew up around the port, off-shooting into the hills.

He figured he would probably need transportation. A rental car would take too long to arrange. Once on dry land, he inquired instead after a moped, the store clerk assuring him it would indeed be able to convey his considerable bulk up the steep inclines of the island. While at the store, Rex picked up a brochure of restaurants, hotels, and bed and breakfasts, and told the man he'd be back for the moped.

His day would entail a systematic search of St. Barts, showing the proprietors the photo of Sabine and, hopefully, tracking her down for a few explanations. With those in hand, he could return to St. Martin, tell the guests she was alive and well, and had decided to leave her husband for whatever reason—and he could then book his return flight to Scotland, case closed.

He started at the café by the dive store printed on Gaby's receipt. "Did you see this young lady in here yesterday?" he asked the handsome bartender in his best French.

"Yes," the Frenchman answered in English. "She was sitting on the terrace with a man. They ordered Veuve Clicquot." He rubbed his thumb and forefinger together. "Big spenders, big tippers."

"Do you happen to know where they're staying?"

The bartender turned suddenly cautious. "Why should I tell you, monsieur?"

Calculating how big a tip the couple might have left him, Rex slid a twenty-dollar bill across the counter.

The bartender slipped it into his jar labeled "*Pourboires*."

"I heard them mention l'Auberge Fleurie." The man shrugged with a self-deprecating smile. "I always listen to what a beautiful woman says, in case I want to find her again."

"Where can I find this place?"

"What is your business with this woman? *Un moment, s'il vous plaît*," he called down the bar to a customer.

"She left a grieving husband on St. Martin. I'm a private detective."

"Ah, how touching—but I am not sure I should give the lovers' secret away."

Rex's muscles flexed in irritation. He didn't have enough twenty-dollar bills to spare and he wasn't about to divest himself of his precious British currency. "The location of the hotel, please," he insisted. "The lady's husband is not a patient man."

"The hotel is up on a hill overlooking Grand Saline Beach."

"Merci buckets," Rex said, pulling away from the bar.

He returned to the moped rental store, made sure of the directions to the hotel, and took off up a rocky hillside, rejoicing in the view of an isolated sandy beach enlacing a turquoise sea. As the road steepened, the feeble motor whined and sputtered in protest. On several occasions it almost expired. Rex ended up abandoning it halfway up the slope among the cacti and wild bougainvillea. "Piece of rubbish!" he muttered, entering the gravel driveway to the hotel on foot.

True to its name, the white façade of the inn nestled in a bower of exotic flowers and tropical trees in bloom, the green-painted shutters open to the beach sparkling far below the cliff. He mounted the steps and, upon entering the hall, came to the reception desk, where he gratefully paused for breath beneath the cooling breeze of the ceiling fan.

"I'm looking for Mademoiselle Durand and her friend," he told the smiling patronne, abandoning his French altogether.

"*Ecossais?*"

"Aye, Scottish. Well-spotted. Was it my red hair or pale skin? Or possibly my accent?"

"*Votre accent, monsieur. Sean Connery, c'est mon James Bond favori.*" The comely middle-aged woman put a hand to her ample chest in a coquettish gesture of adoration.

"He's my favorite Bond too. You canna beat a Scotsman, eh?"

The woman responded with a tinkle of laughter. "*Ah, la chose est sûre, monsieur,*" she agreed.

"Oh, aye—I was asking aboot Mademoiselle Sabine Durand," Rex said, exaggerating his Scots, which he only ever did when he was tired, drunk, or else seeking some advantage with women.

"A charming couple. *Tout à fait charmant.* I put them in *la Miel de Lune.*"

The honeymoon suite—very nice, Rex thought with some irony.

"But you are too late, monsieur. They have already checked out."

"When?"

"But, this morning."

"Do you know where they went?"

"I only know they sailed away on their boat. It is no longer moored in the bay.

"What sort of boat?"

"A catamaran. The *Moonsplash.*"

Sabine could be almost anywhere in the Caribbean by now. Rex made his disconsolate way down the hill and retrieved the moped. Putting it in neutral, he freewheeled down the road into town, relieved to have no further use for it. After dropping it off at the store, he found a vacant table under the awning of a café across from the sleepy harbor. He noticed many of the stores closing for lunch. Consulting the menu, he ordered a beer and *steak-frites. Tae heck with my diet*, he thought. He needed fuel, and fast.

First, though, he should put Vernon out of his misery and let him know his wife was alive.

He went inside to locate a phone, missing the convenience of his cell and regretting not having organized his overseas service better—but then, he hadn't anticipated the island-hopping aspect. "Yes, hello?" he said into the pay phone, having first gotten the code for St. Martin from the waitress. "Is this the Plage d'Azur Resort?"

"Yes, Greg Hastings speaking."

"Rex Graves here. I need to speak with Vernon Powell. Can someone bring him to the phone? I'm calling from St. Barts on an important matter."

"One minute, Mr. Graves." The manager spoke to someone at the desk. "Danielle is going across right now with the message. You best give me the number you're calling from ... Okay. Get back to you in a tick."

Rex watched as his beer passed by on a tray and went after it. "Hold the *steak-frites*," he told the waitress. "I'm waiting for a call."

As it turned out, he could have eaten his steak and fries plus dessert in the time it took for the call to come through. Fortunately, no one else seemed interested in using the phone. Sensibly, they all had cells.

"There is a problem, sir," Hastings informed him as soon as he answered.

What now? Rex asked himself.

"Dr. von Mueller is attending to Mr. Powell as we speak." The manager paused. "He appears to be dead."

"Dead? How?"

"Looks like an overdose. Mr. Brooklyn Chalmers is here and would like to speak to you. I'll pass you on."

"Brook?" Rex asked in surprise. "You're already back from New York!"

"I met with the shareholders Monday morning and got them under control, and flew back out. Rough news about Vernon. Anything I can do?"

"Well, for a start, I need to get off this island."

"You got it. See you at the airfield in one hour."

EIGHTEEN

REX WAS SURE THE von Muellers, who were so correct, would not tell anybody about the sighting of the actress until he returned to the resort. Now that Vernon was dead, he thought it prudent to withhold news of Sabine for now. However, as the Piper bowled down the mountainside runway, he decided he ought to tell Brooklyn that the woman he had clearly been in love with was not dead after all. He waited until they had cleared the airfield and were on their flight path to St. Martin, but Brooklyn spoke first.

"The tower warned me we might run into weather." He checked the altimeter reading. "You could have been stranded on St. Barts."

Even as he spoke, the wind whipped up the waves below them, crumpling the blue tapestry of the sea until it became barely possible to make out the few boats bobbing about like corks on the surface. Rex wondered if Sabine's catamaran was among them. The first few drops of rain had fallen when Brooklyn fueled the plane. Now the wipers worked at a furious pace to repel the deluge.

Rex wasn't too concerned. It was a short distance to Grand Case, and the air-conditioned six-seater aircraft looked solid and new to his untrained eye. All the same, he decided not to distract Brooklyn with the news of Sabine until they landed. "What was going on at La Plage when you left?" he asked instead, anxious to hear details of Vernon's death.

"Pandemonium. Hastings was doing a good job of keeping a stiff upper lip and going about the proper procedure. The ambulance arrived as I left. And there was a tall gendarme with a mustache waving his arms in the air, like he was directing traffic."

"Lieutenant Latour."

"Hopefully the situation will have calmed down by the time we get back."

"D'ye think it was suicide?"

"Accidental maybe. Vernon just wasn't the type to kill himself."

Brooklyn went on to describe the scene at Vernon's cabana as Danielle had recounted it to him. The last track on the CD was playing the Bee Gees, "Nights on Broadway," as she walked in. No sign of a struggle. Everything in its place, down to the re-corked bottle of rum and the pair of tumblers rinsed clean on the counter. Vernon lying on the bed with his arms folded across his chest, naked as a jaybird, a whiff of rum discernible on his pale lips.

A peaceful scene, Rex acknowledged. Except that, if he'd overdosed on purpose, where was the medication and why go to the trouble of doing the washing up?

Approaching the coast, Brooklyn spoke in a series of code into the radio, seeking clearance to land. As he guided the plane through the driving rain over misty hills and depthless valleys, Rex's throat lodged in his mouth. Blurry lights marking the runway rushed up to meet them. Here we go, he thought, his body tensing in preparation. The strip looked terrifyingly short.

The plane swooped down, the landing gear bumped on the tarmac, and they hurtled toward a controlled stop, within a comfortable distance of the barrier. Rex took in a deep breath and exhaled slowly.

"I'm gonna taxi into that hangar," Brooklyn said. "Pascal will be waiting for us in the parking lot. I think we made it just in time. The rain's getting worse if that's possible."

The gale blew so strongly that Rex could barely open the cockpit door. By the time he got to the limo he was drenched through. Pascal slid open the driver partition and pointed to a decanter of brandy in the drinks compartment. He had even brought towels. A gust hurled Brooklyn inside ten minutes later.

Rex poured a tumbler of brandy for his roommate as the car splashed through the rain. "Is all this flying a lot of wear and tear on your plane?"

"The PA-46 is built for long haul. It has a range of 1,345 nautical miles. It's one thousand NMs northwest by west to Lauderdale where I refuel, then almost another thousand to New York, but she can handle it. Depending on when you leave, I could fly you to Miami to get your connection back to Edinburgh."

"Aye, maybe," Rex fudged, thinking the short flight from St. Barts was sufficient experience of a private plane. "Listen, I have news about Sabine I've been waiting to tell you."

"You found her body?"

"No—I have every reason to believe she's alive. Gaby von Mueller spotted her on St. Barts yesterday. That's what I was doing over there. I tracked her down to a hotel where she was staying with a young man, who may be the one she was with when she visited the Butterfly Farm."

"You have been busy." Brooklyn studied his glass, a frown forming between his gray-green eyes. "Alive, you say. Who's the man?"

"I don't know. The woman at the souvenir shop thinks he might have been French."

Brooklyn sat back in the white leather seat. "I can't think of any Frenchmen she hung out with here on the island. I know one who sometimes moors his yacht in the bay at La Plage, but I'm not sure they're acquainted, and he's not her type."

"What is her type?"

"Young. Pretty boy types, judging by the servers she flirted with. I didn't think she was serious about anybody."

"Except you?"

"I thought so. Alive, huh?" Brooklyn looked like a dazed boxer rising in the ring at the last count.

"Did you ever meet her chiropractor?"

"I knew she was seeing one in Philipsburg on a regular basis."

"Aye, well I think she was doing more than getting a spinal manipulation."

"You mean she was sleeping with a quack?"

"I don't think he's a chiropractor at all."

The limo pulled through the gate to the resort and deposited them in front of their cabana. No sooner had Rex scrambled into dry clothes than a knock came at the door and Greg Hastings, the manager, stepped inside, propping his dripping golf umbrella against the wall by the mat.

"Thought I'd come over and fill you in," he said. "Some rather interesting developments. I haven't had a chance to speak to the gendarmes regarding the latest."

"Please ..." Rex ushered him into the living room.

"When you called from St. Barts, I sent Danielle to fetch Mr. Powell for you, as you know. The door to his cabana being slightly ajar, she went in and saw him lying on the bed. Sensing something wasn't right, she drew closer and realized his eyes were open and he wasn't moving or breathing. She ran back to reception and I escorted Dr. von Mueller to the cabana, where the doctor pronounced Durand dead. A CD was still playing when Danielle found him, so he couldn't have been dead long."

Unless someone else reset the CD player just to confuse the police, Rex hypothesized to himself. "Brook told me what Danielle found. It seems odd that a man who was about to take his life would rinse out the glass of rum he presumably used to wash down the pills."

"Well, I don't think he was the one who did that. When I returned to the main building after taking Dr. von Mueller to number 2, one of the staff told me she had seen Sabine there shortly before Danielle found the body."

The manager's account confirmed Rex's suspicions.

"The gendarme is here," Brooklyn informed them.

Lieutenant Latour strutted into the living room. "*Quel sale temps!*" he exclaimed, brushing water off his slicker.

"Foul weather indeed. Mr. Hastings was just telling me we might have a suspect in Vernon Powell's murder."

"*Encore?* Why must he be murdered? Why must everybody be murdered?" Red blotches appeared on the gendarme's face and neck. "Why not an accidental little overdose? Ah, you Sherlock Holmes

160

types! Can you not enjoy our beautiful island without seeing murder everywhere? Well, we will know from ze autopsy what happened."

"We dinna have time. Mr. Powell's wife was here."

"Mademoiselle Durand? *Sans blague!*"

"No, it's no joke. Mr. Hastings just found out from a member of staff. Is it not a wee bit suspicious that Ms. Durand stages her death, mysteriously reappears two weeks later, and within one hour her husband is found O.D.'d in his bed, during which time she mysteriously vanishes again?"

"The lady from maid service came forward and confessed," the manager explained to Latour. "Ms. Durand swore Clementine Guillaume to secrecy with a bribe of one thousand euros."

"Ze maid will testify?"

"She wants to keep her job."

"And do we know where Mademoiselle Durand is now?" Lieutenant Latour looked around the room as though she might be hiding in a corner.

"According to Clementine, she slipped away in the rain dressed in a plastic poncho," Hastings replied.

Brooklyn handed Rex a pair of binoculars. "I just spoke to the security guard. He saw someone fitting that description get into a dingy. My guess is she's on one of the cats out there waiting for the storm to abate so she can get off the island." He turned to the manager. "I borrowed your umbrella. I hope you don't mind."

Rex adjusted the binoculars and focused on a catamaran at anchor in the middle of the bay. The chop obscured the name of the craft, but he watched long enough to decipher some of the letters. A couple of figures scurried about on deck, as though preparing the catamaran for sail.

"She's on that boat," he told Brooklyn, holding the glasses steady so he could see. "The *Moonsplash*. That's how she got here from St. Barts. That's how she left in the first place. The tide was out that night and she swam the short distance to the catamaran, first planting a torn-off piece of her pareo and her ankle bracelet on the beach."

Sabine would have known from her morning rides down Galion Beach where the tide would be at any given point in the day. She had no doubt picked the evening of Paul Winslow's birthday to disappear, knowing the guests would be busy getting ready for dinner.

"They're on the move," Brooklyn said, following the boat with his glasses.

"Lieutenant Latour, can you send a police boat?" Rex asked.

"There's not enough time," Brooklyn interrupted. "The cat could hide out on any number of islands. We need to pick them up before they have a chance to escape."

"What if the police sent a chopper?"

"Not in this weather. C'mon, let's go after her."

"How?"

His roommate laughed as though he had just dreamed up a good game to play. "I have a key to one of the yachts in the bay. It belongs to that Frenchman I told you about. Get something waterproof on. I'll find Pascal. Meet you on the beach in five minutes."

"*Tenez.*" Latour shrugged out of his slicker and handed it to Rex. Clearly, he had no intention of going with them. After a brief hesitation, he offered his cap.

"Thanks."

Rex could not believe he was actually going out on a boat in this weather, but he could not let Sabine get away.

NINETEEN

R EX RAN TO THE beach. Peering through the rain, he saw the *Moonsplash* had not made much progress and seemed to be in difficulty. Pascal and Brooklyn appeared farther down the sand.

"Hop into this old bucket," Brooklyn called to Rex, pointing to a small boat with an outboard motor. "We'll go after them in the *Belle Dame*. Even if Sabine sees people get on the yacht, she'll think it's the owner and his crew."

Wading into the water, Rex climbed aboard and sat huddled on a wooden bench seat while the rain pelted his slicker. Pascal pulled up anchor, and the boat ploughed forward as fast as the little coffee mill of an engine could transport the three of them against the roll of the waves.

Pascal, hand on the tiller, wore a fisherman's knit sweater and hood, which Rex assumed he kept in the trunk of his car when he came to work. The hum of the motor was barely audible above the deafening roar of the sea. The rocking motion unsettled Rex's stomach and he thought he might lose his *steak-frites* after surviving the plane ride. With any luck, the yacht would be steadier.

"They'd be crazy to take that twenty-four footer into open water in a storm like this," Brooklyn remarked, his eyes trained on the catamaran which, after some initial floundering, was making progress toward the mouth of the bay.

"Do you know much about boats?" Rex asked apprehensively.

"I used to race cigarette boats."

"Is there anything you canna do?"

Brooklyn seemed to give the question due consideration. "No," he answered, and grinned as rain poured down his face.

Pascal nosed the dingy behind the *Belle Dame*. Concentrating on maintaining his balance, Rex followed Brooklyn up the fiberglass steps at the stern, across a teak sundeck, and up a steep stairway to the pilothouse. Even at this high vantage point, spray lashed against the wrap-around tempered glass windows. The yacht dipped and reared like a horse on a carousel. Brooklyn hollered down to Pascal and turned the ignition key. The twin engines leaped to life with a tremendous roar. Added to the swaying motion, the smell of diesel made Rex nauseous.

As they left the relative shelter of the bay, pushing out past the island to starboard, the heaving of the sea sucked at the hull, the waves around them roiling masses of foam. Rex felt uncomfortable just watching this stuff on TV from the comfort of his recliner. Would he were there now!

Pascal, who had taken over at the helm, fought with the wheel in pursuit of the *Moonsplash*, which was outstripping them at forty-five knots on a course toward Pinel Island. From time to time, she disappeared from view amid twelve-foot cliffs of gray water. Distantly visible on shore, the palm trees bent sideways in the wind.

"Is this a hurricane?" Rex yelled out to Brooklyn.

"Just a squall. Don't worry, just don't go overboard."

"No chance," Rex said, holding onto the console with white knuckles. "Are you sure we can catch up with them?"

"This is a more powerful boat and Pascal knows these waters. Why don't you go down to the cabin? I'll call when we get near."

"That's okay," Rex said valiantly. How could he ever relate this adventure to Campbell if he had to tell him he'd been throwing up in the head?

Water swept over the bow, splashing the glass. A sailboat out on the ocean was struggling to get its sails down. Pascal called the national police and alerted them to a possible emergency. "Gale force winds up to ninety kilometers an hour off La Plage d'Azur," he reported, reading their GPS location.

The police boat was already on another call, Pascal relayed afterward. All search and rescue boats were busy scooping up fishing vessels and yachts caught in the storm. He tuned in to the local VHF frequency, and they heard the crackling SOS from the sailboat. "Mayday … Mayday," called an American voice. "We're having problems."

Pascal turned to Rex. "Do we go pick dem up?"

"Their mast's gonna snap if we don't," Brooklyn said. "They could end up on the rocks."

Rex thought quickly. He couldn't leave the sailboat and crew to their fate, but he couldn't let a murderer get away either. "Aye, we'd better save that boat," he agreed.

Brooklyn nodded. "If we can get them on course headed into the bay, we can still go after the catamaran."

Suddenly, Pascal pointed. Rex stood on his toes to see over an intervening ridge of waves. The *Moonsplash* had capsized. Two figures bobbed about in the water in life preservers.

"Them first," he told Pascal.

Within minutes, Rex and Brooklyn had hoisted the shivering couple out of the water onto the deck. Not a word was spoken between Brooklyn and Sabine. Rex explained who he was and why he was chasing them. The bedraggled young man with her looked about him like a caged animal.

"I'll take them below," Rex told Brooklyn. "D'you think you can help those people get their sailboat ashore?"

"Aye, aye, skipper."

"Here, take these life preservers in case Ms. Durand and her partner get any ideas about making a swim for it."

Sabine cast Rex a look of disdain. She had the beguiling eyes of a cat, though he couldn't tell if they were more green or more blue. Duke Farley had been right: the girl did look good wet. Her delicate face, nude of makeup, appeared appealingly young. Beneath her life vest, a silk dress molded her small pointed breasts and slight hips. Both she and her partner were barefoot, dripping water as Rex ushered them into a Berber-carpeted cabin with fully equipped galley.

He located a pile of beach towels in a closet and opened the door to one of the staterooms so Sabine could get out of her wet clothes. The man peeled off his T-shirt and waterlogged jeans. He was narrow in the shoulders, his dark hair a dramatic contrast to his face, which was still pinched and pale from shock. Why Sabine had chosen him over Brooklyn, Rex couldn't imagine—but there was no accounting for taste where women were concerned, as he had recently discovered from personal experience.

"I didn't catch your name," he prompted, since it had not been volunteered.

"Jean-Luc Valquez. Thank you for saving us."

It speaks! Rex said to himself.

Sabine stepped into the room, wrapped in a bright towel. "I will never get the tangles out of my hair," she said, tugging a comb through a damp strand. She spoke with a slight London accent. Rex remembered she had worked and been schooled there.

"Perhaps you could rustle up a pot of coffee," he said. "It might take your mind off your hair." He, for one, could use a cup of something hot.

"This is a nice yacht," she said, wandering into the galley. "It's like a mini-condo. Yours?"

"No. It belongs to a friend of Brook's."

"A Frenchman." Sabine waved a packet of French roast at him. "I remember now. An old salt by the name of Fabien."

"How did you get that cut on your wrist?" Rex asked.

"I scraped it on some coral a few weeks ago while I was diving."

"Are you sure it wasna self-inflicted?"

"I have no idea what you're talking about."

"The strip torn from your white pareo has your blood on it."

"Strange."

"Not so strange when one realizes you staged your own death. I suppose you cast the rest of the pareo out to sea once you reached the catamaran."

"Don't be silly."

"Or else Jean-Luc here was onboard all along. You left a piece of your pareo on the beach along with your ankle bracelet."

Jean-Luc collapsed on a stool at the granite breakfast bar and sank his head in his hands. "I had nothing to do with any of this."

Sabine turned on him in a fury. "You bloody idiot. *Idiot!*" she repeated in French.

"She told me to try and escape," he told Rex. "We almost drowned."

"Are you Sganarelle?"

Jean-Luc shrugged in submission. "It was her idea."

"*Veux-tu bien te taire, espèce de grenouille?*"

"Did she just call you a frog?" Rex asked.

Sabine smacked her forehead. "It's the first thing I thought of. I don't mean because he is French. I just meant a slimy little green reptile with bony legs. *Cro-ak, cro-ack, cro-ack!*" she said in her boyfriend's face.

"*Ben, alors? Tu m'emmerdes avec tes histoires!*"

His French moved too fast for Rex to follow, but it didn't sound polite. "How is the coffee coming along?" he asked brightly in an attempt to interrupt the domestic dispute.

The noise and motion of the yacht had subsided. Rex looked out of a porthole near the ceiling and saw they were at anchor in the lee of the island. Pascal must be helping Brooklyn with the sailboat.

"Sganarelle was a sort of code name, I take it?" he asked Sabine. "You could have used Clitandre, but that sounds even more literary, so you transposed the name of the miserly and possessive old man—your husband Vernon—onto the pretend doctor, your lover."

Sabine nodded, a faint smile on her shapely lips. "I'm impressed. How did you figure that one out?" She plunked a mug of coffee and a container of sugar in front of him on the counter.

"I canna take credit. A friend made the connection."

"Surely not the boring Windbag Winslow?"

"That's no way to speak about the man who took you in when you were a struggling young actress."

"Oh, please. I paid rent and, anyway, it was Elizabeth's idea. I don't suppose you have any idea who she is, do you?" She raised her delicate eyebrow at him in defiance.

Rex must have looked blank.

"So, she didn't tell you."

"Tell me what?"

"She's my mother. My natural mother, that is. She gave me up at birth. She was an art student in Paris from a good British family when it was still not respectable to have a child out of wedlock. I was adopted by a wealthy French couple and didn't find out I wasn't their biological daughter until Elizabeth breezed back in my life when I was eighteen and told me. I have never forgiven my adoptive mother for not telling me herself."

"What about your father?"

"The one who adopted me? I was angry at him too, but not as much. As for my natural father, all I know is that he was a French actor and the love of Elizabeth's life. But he is still a *salaud* for running out on her."

"But why Vernon? Why did you marry him?"

"I thought he could take care of me."

"What happened when you went back there today?"

Sabine leaned against the counter with her mug of coffee. "He looked like he'd seen a ghost when I walked through the sliding glass door." She laughed. "The expression on his face was priceless. He was in a maudlin mood, sitting in an armchair listening to Broadway hits and knocking back the rum. I poured one for myself and launched into the role of Abjectly Sorry Wife."

"And you spiked his drink."

"He was pitiful when he realized what I'd done. We were in bed by then. 'What in hell did you put in my rum?'" she slurred in perfect imitation of Vernon's dry American accent.

"'Barbiturates,' I told him. 'Everyone will think you topped yourself.'

"'Bitch. You planned this all along.' Then with his last gasp, he asked, 'Why?'

"'Because you asked for it.'"

Sabine paced the galley. "That's what he said that time he slapped me at the Farley ranch: 'She asked for it.'" Hate transformed her exquisite face.

"There were other ways to get your husband out of your life, you know," Rex told her.

"Not Vernon. Believe me, I tried. He didn't want to be twice divorced. Wouldn't look good on him. And he'd have killed my career stone dead. He was a very vindictive person."

Rex chose to overlook the hypocrisy of that last statement. "And you really thought you'd get away with this elaborate plan?"

The actress gave an elegant shrug of her shoulders. "I might have, had you not interfered."

"People would have figured it out eventually."

"A bit of gossip, some speculation. Nothing provable. The grieving husband drinks himself to death when the wife runs off with a younger man. All the media attention would make me even more bankable. I could have been offered a major movie deal. Now I'll just have to settle for writing a book about my life."

"I'll buy a copy," Rex told her. "I'm sure it'll make for a fascinating read."

A flash of wry amusement illuminated her face. "It will. But maybe you should wait for the movie. I wonder who they'll get to play me?"

"I've always liked Angelina Jolie, myself."

Jean-Luc snorted in derision from where he sat at the other end of the breakfast bar. "You have no sense of reality, Sabine. They will throw the proverbial book at you."

"And you are claiming you had no knowledge of any of this?" Rex asked him.

"I helped her get away from St. Martin. She said she had to leave her husband but was frightened of telling him. I had no idea she was going to kill him. *Quel cauchemar!*" His voice broke on the word "nightmare" as his face fell into his hands.

"His speciality is melodrama," Sabine noted.

"He's an actor too?"

"Yes, of course. Don't you know *anything*? Mainly theatre. We were in an adaptation of *Frenchman's Creek*, where he played the sensitive pirate Aubéry opposite my character, Dona St. Columb."

"A sensitive pirate?"

"It was a stupid play," Jean-Luc concurred. "Based on a stupid novel by Daphne du Maurier."

"It was a huge success at the box office."

"Is that when you two met?"

A frozen silence ensued. Rex deduced he had touched on a sensitive subject. At that moment, the churning vibration of the powerful propellers started back up and they began to move.

Ten minutes later, they were in the bay preparing to embark in the dingy with Pascal. The sailboat was already tightly moored and peaceably cresting the waves, which had lost much of their furor. Brooklyn stood on shore, soaking wet, watching the four of them in the boat. Rex wondered what was passing through his mind as he waited for Sabine, and what sort of reception she would receive from the rest of the guests.

TWENTY

Brooklyn escorted the boat party to the main building, where Greg Hastings met them in the lobby and distributed white bathrobes with La Plage d'Azur embossed in gold on the breast pocket.

"Ms. Durand," he murmured, clearly not sure how to address his previous guest and murder suspect. He looked Jean-Luc over with polite curiosity before making a brief call from reception. "Latour is attending to a traffic accident," he informed Rex, "but will be over as soon as he can. Shall I inform the other guests of Ms. Durand's arrival? I don't think most of them are aware she is alive. I instructed the staff to keep mum."

"Not yet," Rex said, reluctant to have the guests crowding in asking questions while he still had some of his own.

"What do you have to say for yourself?" Brooklyn finally asked Sabine.

"I don't have to answer to you."

The American threw up his arms in disbelief. "I would have thought you have a lot of people to answer to. We all went looking for you. The police were here."

"Am I under arrest?" she asked Rex. "Can you make a citizen's arrest in a foreign country?"

"Lieutenant Latour said to hold you for questioning," Hastings cut in. "In connection with your husband's death. I hope you understand."

"I had nothing to do with my husband's death."

"Ms. Durand," Rex objected. "You confessed on the yacht. Your plan was to resurface months later with your new beau and a watertight alibi and claim your dead husband's estate. You hoped that the notoriety of the case would reignite your acting career."

"What do you mean, 'reignite'?"

"Well, it seems you haven't been in anything lately."

"I've been resting. Mr. Graves put words in my mouth," she told the manager, appealing to him with her cat eyes. "I did not have my own lawyer present. The trauma of nearly drowning when our catamaran capsized..." She put a hand to her throat, ever the consummate actress.

"My poor dear. Perhaps a snifter of brandy?"

"All round," Brooklyn suggested.

"Right." Hastings paced off in the direction of his office.

"Pascal and I swam to the sailboat," Brooklyn informed Rex.

"You're soaked through. But you got her in okay. The passengers must have been right grateful."

"An older couple from Maine. They offered us the use of their St. Thomas villa whenever we like."

Sabine gazed at Brooklyn in overt admiration, probably thinking she would have had a better chance of escape with him. "You don't really think I murdered Vernon, do you, Brook?"

"Jean-Luc is a witness to your confession," Rex reminded her.

"I do not remember anything that was said, except that I had nothing to do with anything," the Frenchman said.

"You remember that much," Rex remarked with a lash of irony.

"I only helped Mademoiselle Durand escape from her husband. You must believe me."

"It's not for me to decide. For now, you must consider yourself a guest of the Gendarmerie."

"Take the young man to my office and keep an eye on him until the police arrive," Hastings instructed Winston, returning with the security guard and a cut-glass decanter. "I left a glass of brandy in there for you," he told Jean-Luc. "There's a divan bed and a blanket. Make yourself comfortable. We'll put Ms. Durand in the small office." The manager led her behind reception.

"How long will I be in here?" she asked Rex, glancing around the functional space. "Can I use the phone?"

"Whom do you wish to call?"

"My father in Paris."

"Go ahead."

Minutes later, from outside the room, he could hear her agitated voice talking in French. "I'll go and see the guests now," he informed Hastings.

A throng of voices arose from the third cabana, occupied by the Winslows. Elizabeth was sobbing on the sofa. "I must go to her," she cried into a handkerchief.

Paul sat beside her, patting her hand. He looked up at Rex. "We saw you come back in the dingy with Sabine. Thought we had all better sit tight and wait for you, though it was all I could do to prevent my wife from running out to the beach in the rain."

"Is it true she had something to do with Vernon's death?" Dick Irving asked from an armchair.

So much for keeping the guests in the dark. The turn in the weather had prompted them to put clothes on, not that the air temperature had dipped significantly. It was probably a psychological reaction to the element of danger posed by the storm—or else they felt uncomfortable and vulnerable being naked in front of the authorities.

"Duke spoke to one of the guards," David Weeks said. "Seems the maid saw Sabine in the cabana at around the time Vernon died."

"Ms. Durand did say she spoke with her husband," Rex confirmed.

"How is she?" Elizabeth asked, her eyes red-rimmed from crying. "She must have got drenched in the storm. What happened to their catamaran?"

"They had to abandon it, but we got her on our yacht, and she was able to get dry."

"I don't know why she left two weeks ago without saying goodbye!" Elizabeth broke down again.

Toni Weeks gently pulled her from Paul's arms and assisted her to the bedroom. Glancing around the open-plan room, Rex noticed the von Muellers installed at the kitchen table with Pam Farley and Nora O'Sullivan. A pot of tea and a half-demolished apple strudel stood on the pine surface.

"Would you like a cup?" Nora asked. "You look blue."

"Aye, I would. I'm just beginning to thaw out. It's the wind chill factor makes a difference."

"How brave of you to go out on the water in this weather."

"Daft," Sean corrected his wife.

"The worst of the storm has passed," Duke Farley commented from the glass sliders. "Wasn't Brook with you?"

"I think he wanted to speak with Sabine alone."

"To think we'd given her up for dead," Nora exclaimed.

"When can we see her?" Paul asked from the sofa.

"I have no wish to see her," Penny Irving said, filling the kettle. "She murdered her husband."

"You think that's what really went down, Rex?" the Texan asked, pulling a cigar from his pocket. "Hell, I can't believe my racquet ball partner is lying dead in a morgue somewhere. Here's to you, buddy," he said, knocking back a tumbler of liquor.

Rex looked across at the Austrian doctor, who sat gravely silent at table. "Ms. Durand mentioned he took a barbiturate with his rum."

"Ah, I see." Von Mueller tugged his white beard thoughtfully. "*Ja*, a barbiturate administered with alcohol would have a compound effect, especially if the person is not used to the drug. It can take effect within twenty minutes."

"And cause death?"

"In a large enough dose. Some barbiturates are very potent. Pentobarbital is used to euthanize animals. Thiopental, another barbiturate, is one of three drugs used in the United States to execute inmates on death row."

"*Mein Gott!*" his wife exclaimed. "Max, you are scaring people! My husband gets carried away," she apologized to the guests.

"I didn't find any drugs in the medicine cabinets next door," Rex assured her.

Gaby was busy scribbling away in a notebook. "How does it work, *Vater?*" she addressed her father.

"An overdose causes heart and respiratory failure, *und* then the person falls into a coma *und* dies."

"Would pentobarbital be used to treat horses?"

The doctor nodded. "For anesthesia *und* euthanasia, *ja.*"

Rex thought it quite possible Sabine had been the one to break into the Sundown Ranch dispensary and had gotten hold of a drug like pentobarbital before she left for St. Barts. Jean-Luc could have kept it until she joined him on the catamaran. Hard to know how deep her leading man was implicated in all of this. Perhaps he was just *acting* the part of a spineless twerp.

"Poor Vernon," Winslow said. "I wonder when she decided to murder him."

"She didn't bring her best clothes or jewellery to St. Martin," Rex stated. "So it's my guess she planned it ahead of time, before she even left the States. There's little question of culpable homicide."

"Culpable homicide?" Duke Farley asked.

"Our term for involuntary manslaughter. No, it was definitely premeditated. On the trips to Philipsburg to see a make-believe chiropractor, she purchased clothes willy-nilly, sometimes in a size too large, to explain away the time she'd been spending with her boyfriend. I found such clothes in her closet."

"Is that when you began to suspect she was alive?" Pam inquired.

"No, although I did think another man might be involved at that point. I thought perhaps she was pregnant and was seeing another sort of doctor. It was my friend from the cruise who suggested that the name of the chiropractor might be a ruse for a secret lover, used to dupe the husband."

"Is that the man we saw on the dingy?" Penny Irving asked, sipping tea at the counter. "He seems very young."

"He's a French actor. They worked together."

"She kept very quiet about it."

"She always was a secretive one," Nora noted.

Penny shook her head. "None of this really surprises me."

"It does make sense when you view it objectively," Rex agreed. "Who had more motive to kill Vernon than his wife? It was the only way she could get his money. Not content with simply leaving him, she wanted to embarrass him with the taint of scandal, perhaps even incriminate him. But to be completely free of him she had to come back and finish him off."

"Sweet Jesus, it sends chills down my spine," Nora said.

"It was Gaby who gave me the first real clue that she was still alive, though I did wonder how a murderer could have carried or dragged a body over all that soft sand when the tide was out."

"So lucky we went to St. Barts," the doctor agreed.

"We wouldna have her in custody now if you hadna, and if the maid hadna returned unexpectedly to Vernon's cabana. No one would have been the wiser until Sabine Durand reentered public life months later, when it might have been too late to prove that she had caused her husband's death." Rex set down his empty cup. "I should like to find out a bit more if I can before Lieutenant Latour takes her in. I'll see Elizabeth on my way out. If you'll excuse me…"

This was the hard part. Confronting a mother's grief suddenly struck him as worse than facing a storm at sea.

TWENTY-ONE

REX KNOCKED ON MRS. Winslow's bedroom door and, upon being invited in, found her stretched out on the bed, in conversation with Toni Weeks.

"I'll leave you to it," Toni said, slipping off the bed.

"How are you feeling?" Rex asked Elizabeth.

"Calmer now. Max prescribed a sedative."

"Vernon told me Sabine took Luminal for anxiety. Did she tell you?"

"I suggested she get on one of the newer types of medication. Barbiturates are potentially addictive. But I suppose she wanted to stick to what she was familiar with."

You got that right, Rex thought. Seemed that Sabine was quite the expert on the subject of barbiturates.

"I thought I'd take her some clothes. You could come with me."

"Do you think she wants to see me?" Elizabeth asked hopefully. "Do I look an absolute mess?"

The usually *soignée* Mrs. Winslow did look ravaged. "This must be verra hard on you," he murmured. "Sabine told me you were her mother. And now that I've met her in person I can see a resemblance." The greenish eyes, the hair color, though Elizabeth's was redder.

"She's very beautiful, isn't she?" she said with a sigh that ended in a sob. "It's not been easy, pretending to be just a caring friend all these years, but we decided it was for the best, to save our families any embarrassment—even though it happened such a long time ago."

"I understand."

"I never forgot her, not for a minute. Every day since I gave her up, I've said a little prayer for her. On her eighteenth birthday, I returned to Switzerland to look for her. The Maison de Lausanne was an institute for young women of society who found themselves in trouble," Elizabeth explained in a voice laced with irony. "It was run by a Madame Bossard. We weren't even allowed to read novels, which were considered to be corrupting. Surprisingly, the director was still alive all those years later, although she was in a wheelchair and a bit senile. Her establishment had reverted to a private house and she was taking in foreign students."

Mrs. Winslow took a deep breath, as though drawing the stamina to continue. "An English girl who was studying French at the university was sympathetic to my plight. She said she'd seen piles of old boxes in the cellar. We went down there. That part of the house hadn't changed one little bit. I was transported in time. It still had the same stone sinks where we used to scrub the bloody sheets by hand in cold water until our knuckles were raw. Most of the deliveries were done on the premises, you see. It may have been an establishment for respectable young women in trouble, but

Madame Bossard made us contribute to the running of the household. I think deep down she wanted to punish us for our sins. The memory made me all the more determined to find my baby!"

Fresh tears streamed down her face. Rex reached for the box of tissues by the bedside and waited for her to continue.

"She had kept all the records of the unmarried mothers," Elizabeth said, after composing herself. "I found my file and discovered that Sabine, whom I'd named Alice, had been placed with a banker and his wife at a smart address in Paris."

"And that was your next destination."

"Yes. I caught the next train out of Lausanne, tracked Sabine down in Paris, and told her everything. She took it very well. We were in a café on the boulevard St. Michel. I remember her saying, 'I knew my mother couldn't really be my real mum. We never got on.' Of course, I should have been sad that she hadn't had a better relationship with her adoptive mother, but I was thrilled. Naturally, she was at a rebellious age, so the idea of our secret communication between Paris and London must have appealed to her creative imagination. Soon after, she came to London. I suggested she try for a job at David's restaurant and then I arranged for her to come and live in our basement flat."

"You confided all this in Paul?"

"Oh, yes. I told him all about the adoption before we were married. We'd been married ten years before Sabine reappeared in my life. I never felt right about having other children. Paul has been so wonderfully supportive."

"That's why you were so eager for me to come to St. Martin and help find out what happened to her. She was so much more than the friend you said she was…"

"We felt the truth would have compromised the investigation. We were sure Vernon had killed her, but you might have felt we were biased if you knew that he was, in effect, our son-in-law. You might have thought we were being over-protective."

"The truth is always best, Elizabeth. It might have saved time. Tell me about Vernon's phone."

"You know everything, don't you? I took it from his cabana while he was out diving. Sabine had asked me to get hold of it if I ever got the opportunity. She said she wanted to get some information off it. I thought it would be a wonderful opportunity while he was out on the boat, but I didn't see her all afternoon. I kept the phone in my purse that evening. It rang while we were on the beach searching for her, an incoming call from abroad. The guards were approaching. I managed to switch it off, then I chucked it onto the rocks. By that time I had a feeling something was terribly wrong. I left it on the beach to point the police in the right direction, to lead them to Vernon."

"You accidentally took a picture of yourself. Fortunately, the police didn't notice."

Elizabeth shook back her mass of red hair. "I'd laugh if it wasn't so pathetic. I was so convinced Vernon had murdered her. I absolutely had no idea it was she who had planned *his* murder all along. She did murder him, didn't she? I wish to God she'd listened to me and not married him. Now her life, her bright future are ruined!"

"They say hindsight is 20-20."

"They also say what doesn't kill you makes you stronger. If I knew who 'they' were, I'd tell them to go to hell."

"Well, I can tell you for a fact Sabine inherited some of her mother's character."

Elizabeth blew her nose and gave a proud sniff. "You had someone taken away from you too, didn't you?"

"My wife, Fiona. She died of breast cancer. She still had so much life left to live. I think the hardest thing for her was knowing she would never see our son grow to manhood." Rex rubbed Elizabeth's shoulder in sympathy. "Are you ready to see her now?"

Elizabeth nodded and accomplished a quick repair of her makeup. "I should go and splash some cold water on my eyes," she said, scanning her face in a compact. "I don't want her to see me in this state."

Paul Winslow stepped into the hall as they were leaving.

"I'm going with Rex to see Sabine," his wife told him. "I wanted to slip out without the others knowing, so I could have some time alone with her."

"Send her my love." Paul took her face in her hands and kissed her forehead. "Chin up." He turned to Rex. "Don't be too hard on the girl."

Rex nodded in understanding. The Winslows had brought him out here to solve a mystery and he had accomplished his mission. The trouble was, it had not turned out the way they had expected. Yet from the moment he suspected Sabine was implicated in her husband's murder, he had had to pursue the case to its bitter conclusion in the interest of justice—which he was morally bound to do by his profession.

He opened the front door for Elizabeth. The rain had stopped, clearing the air and leaving the landscaped grass and tropical plants fresh and invigorated. He, by contrast, felt jaded and in need of a beer. They stopped by Sabine and Vernon's cabana, where Mrs. Winslow picked up a change of clothes for her daughter, and proceeded to the main building. Lieutenant Latour had not yet arrived. The portable TV mounted on the wall at the reception area showed pictures of a fatal pile-up outside Grand Case, caused by the earlier rainstorm. Pierre stood guard outside the small office, watching the news at the same time.

Rex explained his business and, leaving Elizabeth outside the door with a promise to be quick, went in to speak with Sabine.

"Where are the police?" she demanded, leaping from her straight-back chair.

"Are you that impatient to see them?"

"The sooner I'm arraigned, the sooner I can be set free on bail."

"I wouldn't bank on it. It's too easy to disappear off this island."

"It wasn't when I tried earlier. Jean-Luc is such an imbecile. I hope his cell is more comfortable than mine." She indicated the small bare office with a brush of her slim hand.

"The officer in charge was called to an emergency. Then he will see to you."

"I phoned my father in Paris. He's very wealthy, you know. He will hire me the best lawyer and see to it that my *séjour* in prison will be as comfortable as possible. The French will never pronounce the death sentence on me!"

"France abolished the death penalty in 1981, as I'm sure you're aware. If they find a drug like pentobarbital in your husband's system, it will look very bad for you, considering your connection to the stables where the drug was stolen."

Sabine tossed back her head in defiance. "I have no idea what you're talking about."

"Tell me what you know about Monsieur Bijou and perhaps we can work something out."

"What has he to do with this?"

"Nothing specifically, but I suspect him of other murders."

"That cold fish?" She shivered in the bathrobe Hastings had brought her. "Are you referring to the two girls who were found bound and tortured on the island a few years ago?"

"And perhaps others in Amsterdam."

"I have met him a few times. A few weeks ago, he contacted me about doing some publicity for his Diamonds are Forever Club in Marigot and asked me to meet him. I would have gone had I not had a prior engagement with Jean-Luc."

"You're lucky. You may not have left the meeting alive. You're just his type."

"Didn't they find jewels in the victims' sodomized bodies?"

"You seem well-informed."

"The paper said 'raped.' I'm just reading between the lines, knowing what I do about Bijou. But the mayor issued a statement at the time saying the police had reason to believe the murderer had left the island."

"It was wishful thinking. I'd love to put an end to Bijou and his jewel fetishes."

"What would I get out of it?"

"Face space. Every time his name came up in the international news, your photograph would be right there alongside it."

Sabine pouted prettily. "I don't know if I want my name connected to his. It makes me so sick—what he did—what he is."

"There's no bad publicity in your business, you know that. You would be cited as being instrumental in securing his conviction. But I need something solid."

"Well, he did tell me something personal, which is unusual for him because no one really knows anything about him. When he found out my real name was Alice, he said that was his mother's name and that she bore a striking resemblance to me. I looked into his eyes then and it was like staring through the gates of hell. I was fascinated and frightened at the same time."

"His mother's name was Alice Frankel. She married a Henrick van Bijhooven."

Sabine collapsed in her chair. "God! I tried to get Vernon to buy a condo at Marina del Mar. Of course, he was such a cheapskate he wouldn't consider it."

"When news of this gets out, it'll become Marina del Nightmare."

"You are quite funny. Vernon had no sense of humour."

"You don't seem to have a lot of remorse. A jury will want to see tears."

"Don't worry. They will."

Rex had no doubt she would play to the jury. The story of her adoption and insecure childhood would come out, and he wouldn't be surprised if Duke Farley appeared in court to testify to Vernon's physical abuse of her at his Texas ranch, while her biological mother made an impassioned plea for leniency. The French loved drama. "I'll leave you with your mother now," Rex said and he called Elizabeth in. "Ten minutes," he told her.

"Mummy!" Sabine cried, throwing herself into Elizabeth's arms.

"My darling child," Elizabeth said, stroking her long copper-colored hair. "What have you done!"

TWENTY-TWO

STANDING OUTSIDE GREG HASTINGS' office, Lieutenant Latour fondled his mustache with smug satisfaction. "You see, I was right about Mademoiselle Durand not being dead."

"You said she was eaten by sharks," Rex reminded him.

"But not murdered, monsieur. Ze alleged murder victim turned out to be ze murderer. We were both right," the gendarme concluded magnanimously.

"Splendid work," Winslow complimented them both. "But it's been hard on Elizabeth, first thinking her daughter was dead, then finding out she was alive, only to have her taken into custody for murdering her husband."

"We will take her now." Latour signaled to his subordinate. "Is Monsieur Hastings in his office?"

"Aye, he's with Jean-Luc Valquez, Ms. Durand's accomplice. I'm not sure how far he's involved, but I think it's safe to say that Sabine Durand called the shots."

"Zere was a shooting?"

"No—it's just an expression. Incidentally, she appears to know Monsieur Bijou better than most."

"*Alors?*"

"So, you need to bring him in for questioning."

Latour, who already carried heavy purple bags under his eyes, contrived to look even more exhausted. "On what pretext? It has been a long day."

For me, too, Rex thought. "There is no time to waste if this man is in fact the Jewel Killer. I believe I have enough proof for a warrant. He faced charges in Amsterdam for murdering women in exactly the same way he brutalized the two girls here on the island."

The lieutenant sighed in dramatic fashion. "If it is as you say…"

"It would be a feather in your *chapeau* to denounce him."

"If I live to see it. Monsieur Bijou has many persons working for him."

Rex thought of Oscar, the valet-bodyguard. "Well, you can't have Bijou running the island. One of the victims was found across the border on Dutch territory. Even if you don't have the balls here to bring Bijou to justice, at least cooperate with the Dutch authorities."

"Ze balls? What are ze balls we do not have?" Latour asked in all innocence. "It is true we are sadly lacking in resources…"

Rex moved on quickly. "I can give you a profile on his alias, Coenraad van Bijhooven, compiled by Interpol." A slight exaggeration, but the lieutenant looked suitably impressed. "It details his nefarious activities in Amsterdam. I think it makes a strong case against Bijou now that we know for certain he is one and the same person."

"I will do it!" Latour said, standing to attention. "*Ah, oui, monsieur*, leave it to me."

"God help us," Paul Winslow muttered behind Rex's shoulder. "Do you think it'll do much good?" he asked when the lieutenant stepped aside to take a call on his cell phone.

"At the very least, it'll make Bijou feel verra uncomfortable when this gets out. People won't be so willing to hand over their money."

"He may just skip town like he did the last time."

"He can't run forever."

"Marigot?" Latour asked sharply on the phone. "*Mais non, voyons, c'est impossible!*" he protested. "*Mademoiselle Durand est ici sous surveillance.*"

Rex and Winslow exchanged puzzled looks. How could Sabine be in Marigot?

Latour stormed through the lobby, his moustache set in a rigid line.

"Has she escaped?" Rex asked, rushing after him. He had left her with her mother not twenty minutes ago, or however long it had taken him to go back to his cabana to shower and change.

The gendarme gestured to Pierre to open the door to the small office. Sabine looked up from the desk where she was writing a letter.

"*Finalement,*" she said.

Latour turned on his heels. "It is not to be believed. I received a call from ze Marigot police saying Mademoiselle Durand was found dead."

"How can that be?" Winslow demanded.

"Ze police in Marigot did not know we had found her. Someone fitting her description was discovered in an abandoned farmhouse, dead for a couple of weeks, it appears."

"If it's not Sabine Durand, who is it?" Winslow asked.

"Another of Monsieur Bijou's victims," Rex suggested.

"Ze builder for ze renovation, he goes in to check for rain damage. He looks in ze cellar. Ah, ze scene zat meets his eyes and his nose sickens him. He calls ze emergency services *toute de suite*."

"Was there a gem in the woman's naval?"

"A sapphire. Before she died, she was able to write ze letters 'Bij' on ze cellar floor with her blood." Latour donned his cap. "I will take Mademoiselle Durand and her friend to ze station and I will assist in ze arrest of zis monster. *Salut, messieurs*."

As Sabine was escorted from the main building, she slipped an envelope into Rex's hand.

Rex watched while Latour and his sergeant installed Sabine and her wretched-looking friend in the patrol car. He then set foot toward his cabana. Brooklyn sat on the patio staring out to where the umbrellas flopped one by one as the beach attendants passed by, shutting down for the night. There had not been many takers, even after the sun made a brief and reluctant appearance that afternoon. The Irvings, undeterred, were practicing yoga motions in perfect sync on the sand.

"I'm not really one for this naturist culture," Rex confided in his roommate.

Brooklyn shrugged with a smile. "To each his own."

"Sabine gave me this." Rex deposited the envelope on the table. "It's addressed to you."

Brooklyn gazed at it for a long moment before breaking the seal. He reached into his shirt pocket and fished out a pair of reading glasses.

"You need spectacles?" Rex asked in faint surprise.

"A bitch, isn't it? My near vision suddenly deteriorated in the last year or so."

"How old are you?"

"Thirty-seven."

So Brooklyn wasn't perfect after all. Rex didn't need reading glasses, and he was a full decade older than Brook. Nor did his mother, who was in her mid-eighties. He didn't know whether to feel childish disappointment that his hero figure had a physical flaw, or else ignobly pleased.

He went inside for a beer and brought one out for Brooklyn, who threw the letter on the table.

"You know, in spite of what she did, it doesn't really change my feelings for her," he said. "Funny to think we were suspected of having an affair, but since I was still around, no one considered the possibility she may have run off with another man."

"It was a right clever plan," Rex agreed as he sat down. "Are you going to be returning to New York now?"

"No, I'll stick around for as long as she needs me."

"Brook, I wanted to ask you about that woman from Philipsburg you were dating."

"Gerry Linder."

"You just answered my question." So it *was* Geraldine Linder, the murdered tour guide in Thad's report on Coenraad van Bijhooven. When Brooklyn had referred to her as Gerry, Rex had not immediately made the connection. "Are you sure she went back to Europe?"

Brooklyn looked flummoxed. "I don't know. I never heard from her again. One time, after I found out about her involvement with Bijou, I went round to her apartment. I was flying back to the

States and thought I'd say goodbye. No hard feelings and all that. Her landlady said she had gone back to Holland and that some men had been in and cleaned the place out. Why do you ask?"

"She was one of the women murdered on the island two years ago. I have the newspaper cutting. She was found dead in September, missing since the end of August."

"Hell, poor Gerry. I guess I must have missed the story, same as everybody else here."

"It would have come out after you left St. Martin. The paper had to print a retraction clearing Bijou's name. I'm very sorry, Brook."

"You think he had something to do with this?"

"I think he had everything to do with it."

"That's why you went to The Stiletto."

"Actually, I went there to see if he had an alibi for the night Sabine Durand went missing. He did. But she had a lucky escape since it appears he had designs on her too."

"We must have the same taste in women. What's going to happen now?"

"He'll be taken into custody. The latest bit of evidence is quite damning. Anyway, it's not my pigeon. I came to solve the mystery of Sabine Durand and, I have to say, it's been an interesting experience in many ways. I wouldna have missed it for the world."

"Do you think you'll ever return to St. Martin?"

"Who knows?"

The other guests would migrate back to their countries of origin, perhaps to return next summer, but the prize butterfly would no longer be among them. Sabine Durand would grace the gray cell of a prison for many years to come.

"So—looks like you solved at least two cases, Rex. And that's not all." Brooklyn raised an eyebrow in a quizzical expression. "David Weeks said you had a woman visitor while I was away. I'm assuming it wasn't Moira, the social worker in Iraq?"

"No. Her name is Helen."

"A girl in every port, huh?"

Rex coughed modestly. "Just one."

"Hope it all works out for you, buddy."

"I have a feeling it will—but you never know what life will throw at you, do you?"

"You just gotta play it for all it's worth." Brooklyn raised his bottle in a toast.

"Here's to that," Rex said, saluting him with his Guinness.

If you enjoyed reading *Murder in the Raw* by C. S. Challinor,
read on from an excerpt from her next book:

Phi Beta Murder

ONE

From Blackford Hill the volcanic formation of Arthur's Seat resembled a pair of buttocks. People with a more sophisticated imagination likened the shape to a sleeping lion. However, Rex thought Arthur's Seat was aptly named. He enjoyed coming up here to clear his head, especially after a heavy week in court or when he had a problem to mull over, as now. For a minute or two, he pondered the troubling phone call from his son, but it was futile to try and read behind what Campbell had said. It would just have to wait until he got to the States.

Yellow-flowered gorse carpeted the grassy slopes on his way up to the top of the lava rock summit. From this vantage point the skyline of the Royal Mile—Edinburgh Castle, the Highland Tolbooth, and hollow-crowned tower of St. Giles' Cathedral—tood out in crystalline purity, reassuring landmarks that had withstood the test of time and which lent Rex a perspective on the vagaries of life. He had brought Helen up here at Christmas, though the view had not been as spectacular then as on this fresh and sunny spring day. Removing his sweater, he sat on a knoll and watched the swans glide across the reflective blue surface of the loch below, and thought of Helen and their time together.

Dreary rain had bleakened the gray stone of the elegant buildings on Princes Street as they sheltered beneath his brolly, window shopping at the department stores. Her stay at the house in Morningside had been a hoot (to quote Helen). Separate bedrooms, of course—his mother had even put her on a separate floor for good measure. On the occasions Mrs. Graves had left to attend a charity function and the housekeeper went shopping, they had managed a few furtive assignations in his room, reminding him nostalgically of his teenage years when he would sneak a girl up the fire escape. Now that he was in his late forties, such subterfuges seemed ridiculous, albeit necessary in view of his mother's strict Presbyterian ways.

Brushing the grass from the seat of his corduroys, he began his descent down the hill. He had worked up an appetite and was wondering what Miss Bird might have prepared for tea when he caught sight of a tiny, dark-haired figure wrapped in a shawl, waving to him from half way down the path. It couldn't be—and yet, upon their approaching one another, he saw that it was indeed Moira, whom he had not seen in eighteen months.

"How did you know I'd be here?" he demanded, suspecting the housekeeper of divulging his whereabouts. That morning at breakfast he had mentioned he would be going up Arthur's Seat. "Be sure and take yer sweater," Miss Bird had warned. "It can get windy up there." An old joke that had reduced him to giggles when he was a lad...

"We used to climb up here all the time," Moira reminded him. "I spotted you from the Crags."

"Sometimes I walk to Blackford Hill or to the Botanic Garden," he said crossly.

"On a fine day you'd go up here for the view."

Admittedly, she knew him well. They had dated for over two years before she went off to Iraq.

"When did you get back?" he asked.

"Last week."

"Did you bring your Australian boyfriend?" It still irked Rex that she had dumped him following months of silence when he didn't know what might have befallen her, and all the while she'd been seeing this Aussie!

"Don't be daft. I wouldna be chasing you up this hill if he were with me."

"What happened to him?"

All Rex knew was that he was a photographer for the *Sydney News* who had rescued Moira from a pile of rubble after a bombing at a Baghdad market. That and the fact he had blue eyes, a detail she had thought fit to mention in her Dear John letter.

"He went back to Australia."

"Why did you not go with him?"

Her brown eyes avoided his for a moment. "He's married."

"Ah, I see." Rex refrained from asking if she had been aware of that when they first became involved. "Listen, Moira. I have to get home to pack. I'm flying to Florida tomorrow to see Campbell. He seems down about something."

Her sharp features expressed shock and disappointment. "I only just got back."

"Well, I did not know you were coming back. And, anyway, it wouldna've made a difference."

"What do you mean?"

Sticking his hands in the pockets of his pants, he fingered through the loose change. "I'm seeing someone else."

"Who is she?"

"You don't know her."

"And how long has this been going on?"

That was a difficult question to answer. He'd only been intimate with Helen since the summer, after he received the farewell note from Moira, but he had kept in contact ever since he met her while solving his first case.

"Fifteen months," he informed Moira. "I told her about you and said there could never be more than a friendship between us while I was seeing you. Though technically I wasna seeing you since you were miles away in Iraq." As always when stressed, his Scots accent intensified.

"You don't need to sound so het up about it. It was my work that kept me there!"

"It was always about your work, Moira. Aye, I know," he said, warding off her objections with a grandiose wave of the hand. "It's right commendable what you've been doing for the Iraqi civilians and what have you. I respected that and I was prepared to wait. It's you who veered from the path—not I." He didn't even know why he was bothering to have this conversation. It was over between them.

"You have no idea what it's like out there!"

"I don't," Rex conceded. "Look, let's drop it." He stood aside to allow a group of walkers pass on the slope.

"I made a mistake, and I came to tell you I'm sorry."

"Apology accepted. Take care of yourself, Moira." Turning abruptly, he continued down the path.

She grabbed his arm. "Ye canna jist leave," she pleaded. "We need to talk!"

"There's nothing more to say."

"Are you in love with her then?"

Rex looked apprehensively upon Moira's anxious face. "Aye, I suppose so."

A shrewd gleam of triumph lit her eyes. "You don't sound so sure."

He sighed in exasperation. "I don't know what being in love is supposed to feel like at my age." Yet he felt all the right things for Helen: affection, desire, respect—all the necessary ingredients for love once they spent more time together. As it was, he lived in Scotland and she in north central England.

"Rex," Moira said, reaching for his sleeve again.

"Goodbye, Moira."

He strode off down the hill, confident she would never be able to catch up with him, even in her sensible shoes. He blamed her for upsetting his peaceful afternoon. He had wanted to get his thoughts in order before his trip to Florida, and she had thrown them in turmoil. He even found himself wishing she had stayed in Iraq or else emigrated to Australia. He didn't need this extra complication in his life.

ABOUT THE AUTHOR

Born in Bloomington, Indiana, and now residing permanently in Florida, C. S. Challinor was educated in Scotland and England, and holds a joint honors degree in Latin and French from the University of Kent, Canterbury, as well as a diploma in Russian from the Pushkin Institute in Moscow. Her professional background is in Florida real estate. She has traveled extensively and enjoys discovering new territory for her novels.

Visit C. S. Challinor on the web at www.rexgraves.com.

www.MidnightInkBooks.com

From the gritty streets of New York City to sacred tombs in the Middle East, it's always midnight somewhere. Join us online at any hour for fresh new voices in mystery fiction.

At midnightinkbooks.com you'll also find our author blog, new and upcoming books, events, book club questions, excerpts, mystery resources, and more.

MIDNIGHT INK ORDERING INFORMATION

 ### Order Online:
- Visit our website www.midnightinkbooks.com, select your books, and order them on our secure server.

 ### Order by Phone:
- Call toll-free within the U.S. and Canada at 1-888-NITE-INK (1-888-648-3465)
- We accept VISA, MasterCard, and American Express

 ### Order by Mail:
Send the full price of your order (MN residents add 6.5% sales tax) in U.S. funds, plus postage & handling to:

Midnight Ink
2143 Wooddale Drive
Woodbury, MN 55125-2989

Postage & Handling:

Standard (U.S., Mexico, & Canada). If your order is:
$24.99 and under, add $3.00
$25.00 and over, FREE STANDARD SHIPPING

AK, HI, PR: $15.00 for one book plus $1.00 for each additional book.

International Orders (airmail only):
$16.00 for one book plus $3.00 for each additional book

Orders are processed within 2 business days. Please allow for normal shipping time.
Postage and handling rates subject to change.

CHRISTMAS IS MURDER

A Rex Graves Mystery

C. S. Challinor

Christmas in the English countryside—what could be more charming? Not even a blizzard can keep Rex Graves away from Swanmere Manor, a historic hotel in East Sussex. But instead of Christmas cheer, the red-haired Scottish barrister finds a dead guest. Was it a stroke that killed old Mr. Lawry? Or an almond tart laced with poison?

When more guests die, all hopes for a jolly holiday are dashed. Worst of all, the remote mansion is buried under beastly snow. No one can leave. Confined with a killer, no one can enjoy their tea without suspicion and scrutiny. Rex takes it upon himself to solve the mystery, but the most intriguing evidence—a burnt biography of President George W. Bush—offers few clues. Could the killer be the sherry-swilling handyman? The gay antiques dealer with a biting wit? The quarreling newlyweds? Surely, it's not Helen d'Arcy, the lovely lass Rex seems to be falling for …

Each volume in the new Rex Graves Mystery series will feature a unique, exotic setting and diverse characters from around the globe.

ISBN: 978-0-7387-1439-4, 216pp., 5³⁄₁₆ x 8 $13.95